BLUEWATER BAY PROMISE

SERENITY BEACH SERIES

LENA PEARSON

Brookside
Publishing House

Copyright © 2022 by Lena Pearson

All rights reserved.

No part of this book may be reproduced in any form or by any electronic or mechanical means, including information storage and retrieval systems, without written permission from the author, except for the use of brief quotations in a book review.

ISBN paperback, 979-8-9856181-0-5

Cover design by Silla Webb

1

*H*is eyes followed her across the room, watching for an opening.

"Good for you to join us, Ms. Hollis." He called out with an air of authority.

Megan hustled to the rear of the room, hoping Mr. Harris, the big boss, didn't see her. He didn't, but Brandon noticed and made sure everyone else saw her too. Maybe because he was a corporate climbing jerk trying to impress Mr. Harris, or perhaps because she rejected him last night.

"Sorry," she whispered and took a seat in the last chair pulled from the children's library. Meg hated meetings, and especially this one. It was a Friday night, for goodness' sake. Meg, Ciara, and Sharon had standing plans each Friday evening, at the same place and time.

There must be serious news to share, she reasoned. News that couldn't wait until Monday or a horrible announcement that required the weekend for recovery.

Meg checked her phone. Her thick brown hair fell forward. She tucked it back behind her ears and shifted easily in the petite chair. Meg wanted to call the girls and tell them she'd be late, but the meeting was underway and walking out to make a phone call was not an option.

Mr. Harris waved his hand to get everyone's attention. Meg sat in the rear on the edge of her seat, hoping it would be a short meeting. It was midsummer and the humid days made her pine for the beach. She was ready for the weekend.

Outside of her job, Meg loved spending time with her best friends. Ciara owned The Blue Lobster Grill, the most popular restaurant in town. Sharon had returned after her husband suddenly died and bought The Bluewater Inn with the insurance money and has run it for the last five years.

Meg admired how rooted they were in the town and it encouraged her to be less resistant to settling in Bluewater. She took an enormous leap of faith and purchased her first home. It was the first step in getting the stability she lacked growing up with a mom who's profession caused them to move frequently.

Mr. Harris waved his stout arms broadly. "Can I have your attention," he shouted over the crowd. Sweat glistened on top of his head. The group quieted and looked to the front of the room.

"Good evening and thank you for staying. I promise to not keep you long. First, I'd like to say how proud I am of the work you do for this town. The library is organized and we serve our patrons well."

Simon from the circulation desk raised his hand and waved it like a student wanting the teacher's attention. "Sir," he pushed his glasses up the bridge of this nose, "we are very proud to be working at Bluewater Regional Library and are happy to have you here with us." Simon was also a kiss up. It was skill that kept him in the know of the town's happenings.

"Do you bring us good news on this Friday afternoon?" Simon asked.

It was a good question, and maybe that would move the

meeting along. Meg checked her phone. She was already late for dinner.

Sharon and Ciara wouldn't mind, but she did. It was the first warm day in July and they planned to eat on the terrace tonight.

Mr. Harris peered at Simon's badge, which caused him to puff his chest.

"Simon," he said, pointing to his badge, "yes, that is a good question." Simon's face lit up with delight. Mr. Harris clasped his hands behind him.

"I have some news for all of you, but it depends on your perspective whether it's good news."

Meg uncrossed her legs and sat up.

He paced the front of the room, then stopped to scan the small crowd of employees. They were an eclectic bunch of mixed ages and social status. Some were at the end of their careers, others at the start. Many of them long married and some not. There were the part-time workers, but most were full time. Meg was the least of all these since she was the last hired and didn't have tenure. It made her feel vulnerable when she heard rumors of cutbacks, but Brandon reassured her he'd always have her back.

She craned her neck to find Brandon hoping to catch his eye, but he sat at the front of the room dutifully facing his supervisor. Meg knew she didn't have a chance against Mr. Harris. Brandon's sole aspiration was to lead the county's library system and he fashioned him as his mentor.

Meg shifted in her chair restless with the pace of the meeting then raised her hand with a question. She assumed everyone else was too lily-livered to ask. Not that she was usually this bold, but the risk of disappointing her friends fueled her gumption.

"Yes, you in the back." Mr. Harris pointed toward Meg.

She stood, then cleared her throat. "Sir, we appreciate

your kind words, but it's Friday, and we'd all like to start our weekend." Heads nodded around the room confirming what she suspected.

Meg sat back down and tucked her hands under her legs. She usually kept quiet at staff meetings, but this was rudely unplanned and late on a Friday afternoon. While this surprise meeting might be the weekend's highlight for most of her colleagues, she had plans and was ready to end a full week of work.

"Sure, Sure... Meg? Is that right?" he said, pointing in her direction. Meg's face warmed. She didn't say her name and wasn't wearing a huge badge like Simon. There was only one person who knew she hated being singled out and would take pleasure in mortifying her. She'd chat with Brandon later.

"Yes, sir," she answered

Brandon covered his mouth as if to hide a smirk. Meg glared at him and would have pinched his arm if she weren't so far away.

"Good, good. I will cut to the chase. I'm here to say they have recognized our library as a stellar example of how to serve a community's information, education, and entertainment needs. In fact, we are being rewarded with a state-of-the-art facility. One much nicer with better technology than what we have here."

A year ago, Meg had no plans to stay in Bluewater Bay. The beach town had the appeal of an old pair of shoes until she returned for her mother's wedding.

That's when she met Brandon, reconnected with her friends, and serendipitously got a job at the library. Meg felt comfortable enough to buy her first home, and now couldn't see herself living anywhere else.

Meg's rolled her shoulders to relax them. She checked her phone again. It was almost 6:30 p.m. Sharon and Ciara were probably wondering where she was. She'd never been this late before.

"Like they say, hard work gets rewarded," Simon chimed in.

"Sure, but what's the catch?" said another voice from the crowd.

"Well, there really isn't a catch as much as a formality. The formality is we must close this location and merge this branch with a neighboring town's branch. Unfortunately, with the new technology, we won't need as many people to work at the new site."

"Are we all fired?" called out Nancy, a recent widow. The crowd seemed to become bolder with each bit of news.

"No, not fired, but furloughed until we can place some of you."

A collective groan rose from the crowd.

"When will we know?" said Ralph Buckley, a civic minded semi-retired former truck driver who liked to read the noon time stories in the toddler room.

"We're not sure yet. You'll receive a letter in the mail over the next week. Some of you will be placed immediately."

"What about the others?" Brandon asked.

"We will try hard to place everyone, and that's all I know for now."

The crowd grumbled. Shifting chairs reflected the impatience of the group. Mr. Harris tucked his hands behind him, then lifted his chin toward Brandon, who was several inches taller than him, as a signal to stand and take over. Brandon moved to the front of the room and Mr. Harris stepped back.

The questions started immediately. Brandon removed his suit jacket, pushed up his sleeves and attempted to calm the room as Mr. Harris gathered his things.

"This is all news to me too, but I'm sure we'll have

another opportunity to have your questions answered as I know you have many." He shouted over the crowd.

Brandon glanced at Mr. Harris, who walked toward the exit. His square jaw flexed with tension and he rubbed the back of his neck as a glaze of perspiration gave his face a new sheen. Brandon didn't seem prepared for his exit, but he obligingly responded to the crowd's reaction.

"We are appreciative to have heard this directly from our regional director and not a third party." Brandon gestured toward Mr. Harris.

Meg watched Mr. Harris wave and exit, leaving Brandon to fend for himself as the surrounding crowd grew. Meg wanted to help, but she was late for dinner and he embarrassed her one too many times this evening.

Meg picked up her purse to leave and felt a grip on her upper arm. She swung around to see Simon peering down at her through chunky black frames.

"Did you hear about the list?"

Meg pulled her arm from his hold. "What list?"

Simon looked around, then leaned in and whispered. "If your name is on the list, you've got a job and if not —" Simon swiftly moved his hand across his neck in a slicing gesture, "Swoosh!" he said.

"Really!? Have you seen the list?" Meg said. Her hand clenched the purse's handles.

2

Meg walked into the bustling restaurant and looked around for her friends. She replayed Simon's comments while driving to the Blue Lobster Grill. Simon's news rattled her more than she expected. She'd believed in Brandon and his promise to look out for her.

He was the reason she got the job as a favor to her mother's husband, the Colonel. Now she wasn't so sure. Simon didn't help matters, since he didn't see the list for himself. Should she even believe him?

Meg finally spotted her friends. Ciara waved her over to the table. Sharon met her with a cheerful smile that sparkled against her honey tan skin. The hostess led Meg to the corner table.

"What happened to dinner on the terrace?" Meg asked.

"It's a popular spot tonight. I figured we have the rest of the summer to eat out there," Ciara said.

Meg pulled out a chair. Sharon scooted over to make room in the cozy space, then held Meg's purse until she sat down.

"What took you so long?" Sharon asked.

Meg rolled her eyes. "You don't want to know."

Ciara's eyes brightened with curiosity. "Yes, we want to know. You're never late."

"Sorry, I know I should have called, but I didn't expect the meeting to run that long."

"Oh, one of those?" Sharon chimed in.

"I know. Can you believe they called a meeting on a Friday afternoon?"

"What did they say that couldn't wait until Monday? I would never hold up my employee's weekend like that," Ciara said.

"Well, it wasn't good news. In fact, not sure if you've heard, but the library is closing to make way for the library of tomorrow," Meg said, lifting her hands to make air quotes. She looked around the room. It was filled with the regulars, which comforted her, considering the coming changes.

Ciara rolled her hazel flecked eyes. "Really? That's what they told you, huh?"

Meg picked up the menu. She knew the selections like the back of her hand and looked out of habit. After placing the menu back on the table, Meg looked at Ciara.

"What do you mean? You know something different?" Meg asked.

Sharon pointed to parts of the menu and mumbled about calories, carbohydrates, and proteins. She pulled out her phone and tapped through her app. Sharon tracked her foods to lose the stubborn fifteen pounds she'd gained after her last breakup.

Ciara stood.

"Where are you going?" asked Meg.

"One of the cooks called out tonight and I need to make sure the kitchen is okay. One perk of being the owner, always working."

Ciara gave a weary smile that pushed up her full cheeks.

She stood and walked to the kitchen while Sharon and Meg glanced at each other.

"She works so hard. I wish she'd take a vacation," Sharon said.

"I know, but she wouldn't be able to stay away for more than an hour without finding an excuse to get back here. As hard as she works, this is Ciara's happy place."

"You're right."

Sharon went back to her calorie counting while Meg poured herself a glass of water from the pitcher on the table. "Do you know what you're having tonight?" she asked after putting the glass down.

"The shrimp scampi looks good, but I'd have to run twenty miles to burn off all of those carbs." Sharon chuckled.

"That would be a lot of running." Meg chuckled.

Sharon's eyes shifted above Meg's head, and Meg turned around to see Brandon approaching the table. His lean frame maneuvered the packed tables until he reached theirs.

"Hey, ladies. Mind if I join you?" Brandon pulled out the chair that Ciara vacated and sat down. Megan moved over to make room and greeted him with a peck on the lips.

"Hey, Sharon. How are things at the B & B?" Brandon asked.

Sharon's flashed a hint of irritation. "It's called an inn and things are great."

"Inn, B & B, they're all the same," Brandon said and waved a dismissive hand.

Sharon pressed her lips together, forming a hard line. She flipped the menu over to look at the drink section. When Sharon was hungry her tolerance slipped to all time lows.

Brandon turned to Meg. "Did you order yet? I'm starving." He picked up the menu and thumbed through it.

"How did the rest of the meeting go?" Meg asked.

He smirked. "Lots of questions, concerns, and complaints.

I saw you duck out the back door and leave me to fend for myself. You're supposed to be there for me."

Sharon covered her face with the menu. Meg sensed major eye rolls.

"I know, I know, but Fridays are girl's night and we always have dinner at the same time. I wasn't expecting that meeting. It made me late."

"Sure, Meg, but what's more important? What about us?" He picked up Meg's hand and rubbed her knuckles. She relaxed under his touch. He knew her weak spots.

Sharon coughed from behind her menu at the same time Ciara returned with appetizers. She sat them in the center of the table.

"All is good in the kitchen... Oh, hello, Brandon."

"Hello, Ciara. What's up in the kitchen? A complaint from a customer about a dish?" He smiled and helped himself to two hot wings.

Ciara forced a smile and gave him a clap on the back. Brandon dropped a wing on the napkin and rubbed his back.

"Brandon, you're such a funny guy and you're sitting in my chair." He moved to the chair on the other side of Meg and draped his arm over her shoulder. "Sorry about that," he said and picked up the wing from the barbecue stained napkin.

Sharon and Ciara thought Meg could do better. While they tried to respect her relationship, it was clear how they felt about Brandon. Ciara once described him as self-centered while Sharon swore it was illegal to have an ego that big; but Meg appreciated his confidence. He made her feel safe. Ciara even offered to introduce Meg to one of her brothers, but she wasn't interested.

Ciara sat in the chair and placed a few wings on her small plate.

"I'm sure Meg has filled you in about the library and the

good news about finally bringing us the technology that the old eyesore of a building has been lacking."

Meg shifted in her chair. She wanted to ask about *the list*, but wasn't sure if it was rumor or real. "Well, no, I didn't finish sharing. You kind of interrupted before I could tell them, and I don't think I'd call it good news. Some employees may not have jobs next week."

"You have nothing to worry about. The director confirmed I'll keep my job and I'll put in a good word for you," said Brandon. Meg felt a selfish sense of relief, but worried about the others who depended on the job for their livelihood or social connections.

"I'm sure your job is secure, Meg. You've been there a while, and I heard Nancy is ready to retire," Sharon said, still eyeing the menu.

"Well, I think Meg's right to worry." They all looked at Ciara. Meg leaned in, slipping from under Brandon's heavy arm.

"What do you mean?" Meg asked, interested to hear what Ciara had to say.

"Unfortunately, my brother Kevin, the mayor," Ciara said with sarcasm, "during a few family dinners has mentioned meetings with developers who have big ideas for our town. Things like outlet shopping, a big board walk, maybe gambling."

Meg's eyes grew enormous with surprise. Sharon dropped the menu and asked, "Outlets like the Christmas Store?"

"Sharon, that's not good for our community. We've done fine without big box stores and all the noise, pollution, and traffic it brings. I think we've got a good life here in Bluewater Bay and we should protect it," Ciara said and pushed several red floppy curls out of her face.

Meg tucked her layered bob behind her ears after watching Ciara's hair fall out of place.

Brandon crossed his arms. "I don't know about that, Ciara. It doesn't make much sense. Where would an outlet mall go? The library is too small to put a bigger one in its space. How on earth will an outlet mall fit there?" Brandon never let an opportunity to challenge Ciara and it was not in her nature to let things go by.

Ciara tapped her lip and looked around her cafe. It was full of chatting patrons enjoying dinner out. "Well Brandon, like you, I don't have the details but mark my words, the library's move has nothing to do with a fancy new one. Sorry to burst your bubble." Ciara smirked, then turned to Meg and Sharon. "Are you ladies ready to order for our ladies' only dinner?". Ciara emphasized ladies then looked at Brandon.

Meg side glanced Brandon. A frown replaced his grin. He pushed his chair back and stood up.

"I can tell when I'm not wanted. Enjoy your food, ladies and Ciara." Brandon leaned down and kissed Meg.

"Good talking to you, Brandon," Ciara said.

"Bye, Brandon." Sharon waved.

Brandon walked around the table. "Enjoy," he said and moved toward the bar.

Ciara watched him settle onto one of the bar stools. "I should've guessed he wouldn't have left that easily."

Sharon pointed to a line on the menu. "I'm having the shrimp scampi."

"What about the calories?" asked Meg

"I'll just have to run the twenty miles tomorrow." Sharon grinned.

"Really?" said Ciara

"No, I'm just kidding. Not with these knees."

"I think I'll have the same, but with a glass of wine," said Meg

Ciara waved over one of the waitstaff "Please tell the kitchen to whip up two plates of shrimp scampi and I'll have my usual."

The lanky young man with red spiky hair scribbled the order on his pad of paper, then looked at each of the women. "What can I get you to drink?"

Meg pointed to the wine menu. "I'll have the house wine."

Sharon gestured toward the pitcher on the table, "I'll stick to the water."

Ciara handed him the menus. "Bring another pitcher of water for the table. I don't drink on the job." She smiled at her eager employee.

"I'll bring your drinks right out." He took the menus and moved to the next table.

"I've never seen him before… a new hire?" Meg asked.

"Yep, here for the season. I think he's a student at Bay State U… nice kid. But that's not what I want to talk about."

Sharon rolled out the napkin and placed it on her lap. "Okay, we're all ears."

Meg scooted closer to Ciara. She was glad to be spending time with her friends, but wished Brandon had stayed.

"I wanted to wait until Brandon left before telling you everything I overheard from Kevin. You must promise not to say anything… especially to Brandon."

Sharon nodded, and Meg winced.

* * *

Ciara lowered her voice to just above a whisper, causing Meg and Sharon to crowd in more.

"Why are you whispering?" Meg asked between sips of wine.

"Well, the truth is I have details about the proposed development, but it confirms nothing, and it can't go any further than this table... swear?"

Sharon held up her hand. "On my dead husband's grave."

Meg's eyes widened. Ciara opened her mouth to speak, but stopped.

"What? You all know how I feel about my dear Charlie, but that's another story," Sharon said with thinly veiled sarcasm.

Ciara shook her head. "Okay. So here's what I know—and Meg, you can't utter a word to Brandon."

"Pinky swear." Meg wiggled her small finger at them.

"So, Kevin has been having dinner at our mom's house and talking about the revenue and all the tax money some towns up on the North Shore have been making behind new development."

"That's true, but they're not on the Cape and are larger towns with more people. It's a totally different situation."

"You're right, Sharon, but that's not how my brother sees it and he has the backing of some of the town's officials."

"What would that do to our town? The big bullies have started with closing the library and now I may not have a job and some of my colleagues too," said Meg.

"Isn't development supposed to bring new jobs?"

"I guess ultimately, but it also takes away business from places like mine. And with the scale of this deal, it looks like they'll need plenty of space to build," said Ciara

"So, where are they going to find the space? Bluewater is a small town and we're not the North Shore."

"They'll start with spaces like the library and many folks don't know it, but there's a huge plot of land behind the library that leads flat out to the beach. Oh my goodness, they don't have to move us. We could build new in the same space!" said Meg.

"Shh!"

"I have to tell Brandon so he can tell the director, and that will save our jobs."

"Meg, that's not how it works. I'm sure the director is aware of the space. And like I said theses details can't go further than this table. You have to promise me to not tell Brandon."

"But, he can help us."

Sharon waved a painted pink nail at Meg. "I don't think he'd believe us and his job is secure. Did you hear him? He didn't seem all that sympathetic."

Meg blew out a short breath. "I guess you're right, but I don't think you two give him enough credit; he cares about the library staff."

"Meg, please, promise you won't say anything. Like I said, nothing is confirmed and I don't want rumors to spread. As much as we love Bluewater, it is a small town."

"Okay, Ciara, pinky swear." Meg held up her finger and looped it around hers.

Steamy plates of shrimp scampi were placed on the table before them as if from thin air. Ciara jerked her head up. "How long have you been there?"

"Sorry, I didn't mean to startle you. The plates are hot and I had to place them down," said the server.

"Boy, he's efficient and quiet. Maybe he should work for the FBI," Meg joked.

He placed a grilled mushroom burger platter in front of Ciara, and left with a quick turn of his red spiked hairdo.

Ciara picked up a few fries to nibble.

"I don't know about you, but I'm starving." Sharon pierced a mound of pasta with a fork, and twirled it.

Meg's food smelled and looked delicious , but her appetite dissipated under the worry of losing her job, the coming development and those old feelings of being uprooted. A wave of nausea overtook her senses. She needed air. "I'm sorry, ladies, but it's been a long day. Would you mind if I took dinner to go?"

"Sure, I'll grab a box for you. I need to see how things are in the kitchen, anyway." Ciara stood up and walked back to the kitchen to check on her chef and staff. She returned in minutes and handed the box to Meg. She peered a little closer at her friend.

"Are you okay?" Ciara asked.

Meg didn't want to worry her friends. She noticed Sharon's look of concern too.

"I'm fine. I guess the work week took more out of me than I thought."

Sharon nodded her head then placed her hand over Meg's. "Please let us know if you need anything, okay.

"Will do." Meg pushed up the corners of her lips into a weak smile.

Ciara packed her food into the box and handed it to Meg and gave her a reassuring smile.

"You know the elections are coming up and a new mayor might not support the development. "

Meg patted the full box ."That would be great. Is this Kevin's last term?"

"No, and I think he's planning on running again."

Sharon took a sip of water and sighed with satisfaction. "This pasta is delicious, and maybe we're assuming too much. I mean, would it be so bad to have The Christmas Store in our own backyard?"

"Now, that's another perspective and on that note, I'm heading home." Meg picked up her box, purse, and hugged her girlfriends before leaving.

On the way out the door, her phone buzzed and she pulled it from her bag. It was Brandon.

What did he want?

3

Meg balanced the box of pasta with one hand and tapped the screen with a free finger.

"Hey, Brandon, I'm on my way home." She said into the phone and waited for his response.

He sounded tipsy, no doubt from more than a fair share of drinks at the bar. He must have seen her leave.

Meg wedged the phone between her ear and shoulder so she could rummage through her purse for the car keys while listening to his petition to drop by her house. She wasn't up for company , especially drunk company, but Meg felt obligated to be available for him.

"I'm kind of tired, but sure you can stop by for a minute. Okay, see you soon." Meg sighed then dropped the phone back into her bag and found her keys sitting on top of the bag clutter. She hoped Brandon didn't have the same intentions as last night. Meg knew how persistent he could be.

They'd been dating only a few months and the plan was to keep it low-key since they worked together, but most folks caught on pretty quickly.

She promised herself that she wouldn't become intimate

with anyone until she knew the relationship was going somewhere. Brandon hadn't given her that reassurance, but he had potential.

Megan turned the corner to the side parking lot and finally spotted her used by trusty Accord. Another car pulled in beside hers, leaving barely enough room to open the door, let alone squeeze in. Meg walked to the passenger's side, opened the door and put her dinner in the back seat.

She wiggled over to the driver's side, and settled behind the wheel. Meg put the car in reverse and in a few turns drove out of the small parking lot and down the main street toward home.

Pockets of tourists walked toward the beach, which provided a front seat to beautiful sunsets. Meg felt lucky to have that experience in her backyard.

She slowed to park in the reserved spot in front of her townhouse. Meg was proud to have her own place after a childhood of moving and living in one rental after another. Her mom gave Meg and her sister the best she could, but single parenting was a hard and expensive job.

Meg turned the key to enter her townhome and heard the meowing before she opened the door. Trixie raced down toward her and nearly slammed into Meg's legs.

She loved her cat, although she was more like a guard dog with passive aggressive tendencies. It was clear to Meg when Trixie didn't like a person. Sometimes it was downright dangerous. Trixie's flying sneak attacks from her cat tree caused a few people to flee from her place.

"Hey, Trixie girl." Meg hung her purse on the hook then kneeled down and scratched under her chin. Trixie purred her approval.

Meg walked into the kitchen and Trixie followed. "I'm sorry to be gone all day. We had a late meeting then I went to meet the girls."

Trixie sat on her hinds swaying her tail back and forth while watching Meg move around the kitchen.

She opened the fridge and slid the box inside. There was plenty of space since grocery shopping was on her list of things to do this weekend. In fact, it was on her list last weekend, but she never got around to it.

Trixie stared at Meg then shifted her gaze to the bowl by her foot.

She looked down. "Wow! You ate all of your food. You must have been hungry."

Meg made it a point to fill her bowl every morning. There was usually some left over in the evening. She picked up her calico baby and rubbed her head.

Trixie purred and licked at Meg's fingers with her scratchy pink tongue. The sauce from the shrimp scampi leaked onto her hand from the box. She licked several more times before Meg placed her back on the floor.

"Yes, it's shrimp… I should have a can of shrimp flavored mix for you right here in the cabinet."

Meg opened the tall pantry and took out a can of meow cat mix, but Trixie sat in front of the fridge. It was clear she wanted Meg's meal.

But meg was cautious about giving Trixie human food. She learned her lesson with Ming. They lost their dear Ming not long ago. Meg missed her Siamese fur baby.

She swore Ming's insistent eating of leftovers from the trash led to her illness. Meg picked up Trixie's bowl and opened the can of shrimp flavored cat food. Trixie jumped on the counter and pawed at Meg's hand.

"Okay girl, I'm moving as fast as I can. Give me a chance."

Meg scooped the meal into Trixie's bowl, then watched her take steady bites. Meg's stomach growled. Her appetite returned. She went to the fridge to take out a portion of her own pasta dinner and sat at the kitchen table when a trio of knocks sounded on the door. Trixie's head popped up from her bowl.

"Oh, that's just Brandon. Finish your meal."

Meg got up from the kitchen table and walked to the door. Another round of knocks quickened her walk.

"I'm coming, I'm coming." Meg unlocked the door to find Brandon, who stood in the doorway, hands shoved in his pocket, and a grin smeared across his face.

* * *

"Hey Meg, what's up?"

The smell of beer wafted from his mouth. Meg stepped aside, to let him in. He came in and surveyed the space as if he'd never seen it before.

"You know this is only the third time I've been to your place and second time inside, not that I'm keeping track or anything."

And I've been to your place once, but I'm not keeping track either, she thought.

Trixie strolled in from the kitchen paused and sat on her hinds. She gave Brandon a peculiar stare, got up, and walked away.

"Pixie, right?"

"No, it's Trixie, and if she hears you saying it wrong, she'll use your leg as a scratching pole."

Brandon's eyes grew to the size of silver dollars, Meg chuckled. "I'm joking. Do you want to sit down?" She gestured toward the sofa.

"Sure. Thanks. It's really cozy in here. I like it."

"I like it too. It's my first time owning a home."

"Really!? That's cool. I thought about buying something, but wasn't sure about settling down in this town."

"It was a no brainer for me. My family moved around a

lot before settling in Bluewater. It's the only place that's ever felt like home after all those years of instability. I guess it's part of the reason I'm having a hard time with the library closing."

Brandon grabbed the remote from the living room table. "That's a sweet story," he said with indifference and flicked on the TV. Meg grimaced and watched him recline on her sofa and flip through the channels.

"Got anything to drink?"

Meg paused before answering. "I have water—haven't been to the grocery store , lately."

"Water? No beer, no juice?"

"Nope. Sorry, that's it." Meg wanted to be hospitable, but she wasn't feeling cheery, nor was she inclined to play the ultimate hostess at that moment. The news of the library got her in a mood, and it wasn't Brandon's fault. He might not be an easy person to entertain, but she'd do her best to be hospitable.

"Let me see if there's something I overlooked." Meg got up and walked to the kitchen. Trixie returned and followed her. She jumped up onto the single stool, waving her tail back and forth with a questioning look on her feline face.

"He won't be here long, and I know he's in your seat, but be nice."

Trixie jumped down as though satisfied with the answer, then sashayed out of the kitchen.

Meg opened several cabinets until she found a long forgotten bottle of Tang. She checked the expiration date. It was good for another month. She took out two glasses, measured the powder into them, filled them with water and ice, and carried the filled drinks to the living room.

Brandon stretched his long legs and crossed them at the ankle. His thumb rested on the arrows of the remote control, ready for action. Meg spied Trixie at the opposite end of the sofa, licking her paws. Meg put the glasses down on the coasters she pulled from the shelf beneath the table.

"What's up with your cat? She's been eyeing me like I'm her next meal."

Meg smirked, shooed Trixie off the couch and waved a scolding finger at her. "That's not good manners, Trixie girl." She turned to Brandon and gestured toward the drinks.

"I found some Tang in the cabinet. It must have been left over from my nephew's visit."

Brandon picked up the glass. He gulped it down, plopped the glass back on the table the patted the space on the sofa beside him.

"Why don't you come a little closer. I won't bite— unless you want me to?" He wriggled his thin brows at her.

Meg pressed her lips together then forced the corners to curl up. She couldn't believe they were heading toward a repeat of last night. Either he had serious short term memory loss or his ego was too large to accept rejection. Meg sat on the opposite side of the sofa not wanting to rebuff him outright.

"Well if you don't want to sit near me do you have any snacks?" He asked then belched.

An invisible cloud of beer gas floated to her end of the sofa. She covered her nose and if she wasn't already turned off that surely did it.

Brandon patted his tummy, "My bad, I should've had something to eat. Got anything?"

"I'm sorry, Brandon, but I'm fresh out of food and haven't been to the store in a while, but I'm happy to share my shrimp scampi dinner with you."

Trixie's head whipped in Meg's direction as if she committed betrayal. Are there awards for best in cat drama? Meg shook her head. She watched Trixie saunter over to her cat tree and leap to the mid level. Meg turned her attention back to Brandon whose thigh was now touching hers.

"What are you doing?" She exclaimed.

He quickly slipped his arm over her shoulder and pulled her in. "You looked like you were getting cold over here, so I'm here to warm you up." His voice was low and coarse.

Before Meg could respond Brandon pressed his lips hard against hers and grabbed at her chest. Meg shoved him throwing herself off balance. She fell to the floor with Brandon landing on top. Meg couldn't breath or see beyond him and squirmed beneath his weight.

"Get off me!"

"Argggh!" He screamed as he reached up to his head then rolled onto the floor. His hair was suddenly weird, fluffy and orange.

OH CRAP! Trixie did another flying sneak attack. Meg jumped up and attempted to pull Trixie off Brandon's skull, but her claws were in and she wasn't letting go.

"I'm sorry, I'm sorry. This is not like her." Meg apologized.

"Get your stupid cat off me!" He yelled while kicking and toppling over the cat tree. Trixie immediately jumped off then shot like an arrow to one of the back rooms.

Brandon rolled onto his back then sat up against the sofa. There were scratch marks where Trixie dug in her claws. A little blood seeped from a few of them.

"I'm so sorry…so so sorry. I have some alcohol and band aids. What do you need me to do?" Meg said gently padding around his forehead. The scratches weren't as deep as she suspected. He'd gotten off pretty well.

Brandon smacked her hand away. "What you need to do is euthanize that crazy cat." He said then reached into his pocket and pulled out a wad of tissue. A condom wrapper fell onto the floor. Meg grabbed it and held it up for him to see.

"It looks like my crazy cat knew what you were up to and someone may need to be neutered ."

He had it coming to him and Trixie was only trying to protect her. Meg would give her an extra treat for bravery.

Brandon snatched the square foil wrapper from Meg's finger tips and shoved it back in his pocket. He rose to his feet and faced her. Meg stood firm.

"Do you really think that was for you? You've been clear about…" he paused to make air quotes "saving yourself. I just thought we could smooch a little. What kind of animal do you think I am?"

Meg shrunk back. Did she misread what happened? Brandon respected her boundaries in the past. He's done so much for her. Meg felt her chest tighten and uncertainty scrambled her thoughts. Meg knew he'd always be in her corner and needed him as a friend.

"You're right. I might have overreacted. It's been a long day and I should have told you it wasn't a good time to visit. It's my fault, and I'm so embarrassed about Trixie." Meg looked away unable to meet his gaze. Now she wasn't so sure about what she thought happened.

Brandon rolled his eyes and rocked back on his heels. "I guess I should forgive you." He said and patted Meg's shoulder.

Meg gave him a weak smile and pushed back the edging unease that bubbled from her gut.

Brandon touched one of the scratches along his hair line. It was already less red. "Well, I better get out of here before Pixie decides to return for a repeat performance." He said making his way toward the door.

"You're leaving?"

Meg swore to Ciara that she wouldn't say anything to Brandon about the details of the development, and would keep her promise, but she was curious about the list that Simon mentioned.

"Wait, I wanted to talk to you about something important... about the job."

Brandon stopped then scratched the back of his neck. "What about the job?"

"Well, during dinner tonight, after you left, we talked more about the library closing, development and people losing their jobs. I heard there was a —."

Brandon held up his hand "Stop, before you go any further. I hate to say this, but your friend Ciara has no clue about the plans for the library. Those decisions are being made by important people in the regional offices, with firsthand information. She doesn't have that kind of access. I'd be careful about listening to her. You're smarter than that," he said before knicking her on the chin with his fist.

Meg's face warmed. There had been enough confusion for the night and she'd ask him later about keeping her job. But, she didn't like his disregard for Ciara.

"I think she knows a lot. Ciara is pretty informed."

Brandon sighed. "But she's not... trust me." He pulled out his phone, glanced at the screen, then tucked it back in his pocket. "I better go. The stores will close soon and I'm hungry. Thanks for the Tang."

Meg followed him to the door and opened it. Brandon stepped over the threshold then turned back as if he'd forgotten something.

"If you have any more questions that come to that pretty little head, ask me first," he said, then pecked her on the lips. Meg watched him skip down the few steps before getting in his truck to drive away.

She closed the door and headed back to the kitchen for a few bites of her previously untouched dinner, but her appetite had waned during Brandon's visit. Meg ate what she could, stored the rest in the fridge then settled on the couch to catch the end of her favorite cop show. Trixie reappeared from her hiding place, hopped up on the sofa and kneaded her paws against Meg's leg.

Meg rubbed her head. "You know, Trixie, that wasn't a nice thing you did. Brandon's not a bad guy. You have to give him a chance."

Trixie yawned then rested her head against Meg's leg. Meg took a cue from her furry baby, got up, stretched then fetched her purse. It was nearly her bedtime. She took her phone out and put it on the charging port when a text from Ciara popped up.

"Turn on Channel 12 news. Told you so!"

4

Meg barely slept. Last night's news report kept her on her couch later than usual, and when she finally got to bed, she twisted and turned through the night. Ciara's insider knowledge proved right.

The local news reported a story about land in Bluewater being sold to developers for a mall. It wasn't conclusive, but enough of a possibility that it caused Meg to worry about what other information she didn't know and if she would work for the library again.

Meg rolled out of bed and tramped to her kitchen. She turned on the coffee pot and shuffled through her shelves for sugar.

"Ugh! I've got to go shopping."

She liked milk and sweetener in her coffee. Enough to qualify it as a latte, but she'd have to make do with creamer alone this morning. Meg held her steaming cup not sweet enough coffee, walked into the living room, and sat in her rocking chair.

The cherry wood rocker had been in her family for a couple of generations, and she was lucky enough to get it from among her grandmother's things before the estate sale. Trixie was up early as usual, stretched out lazily in the front east-facing window to catch the warmth of the morning sun. She made life look so easy. But I guess if all I had to do was eat, nap, and catch morning rays then life would be sweet, Meg mused.

In the past, Meg worked Saturday mornings at the library's circulation desk. And when they needed her, she helped out in the children's section.

If she had to choose her favorite part of the job, it'd be working with the children. Research was a close second. But there would be none of that today and she wasn't sure when things would get back to normal. It was weird to have this free time on a Saturday morning.

Meg settled into the chair with her morning cup of Joe certain she'd get used to it. Besides, it likely wouldn't be long before she was back to work. Brandon promised he'd make sure she had a job and Meg depended on it.

She took a couple of sips of her unsweetened latte and decided she needed to head to the grocery store. Meg could make do with many things, but bad coffee was not one of those. She added the mug to her growing dish pile in the sink that she'd get to tomorrow.

Meg showered, dressed, and was out the door with her grocery sacks. She pressed the key fob to open the door of her older model, but reliable sports coupe. It started with an easy hum and she was on her way.

Meg liked to shop in the neighboring town since it had the combined retail and grocery store where she could buy food and pick up things for the house. Its convenience made the case for a little more development in Bluewater, she thought.

Meg pulled off the two-lane road into the large parking lot that was filled with Saturday shoppers. Her plan was to make it a quick trip of getting what she needed and being on her way. Meg wasn't a fan of large crowds, which was one of the reasons that spurred her to plant roots in quiet Bluewater. It was the last town her mom settled with Meg and her sister, Pamela, and she was comfortable there.

Meg made friends easily; a skill she mastered from years of moving from one place to the next. Pamela was less interested in finding new friends in new places. She preferred the anonymity of larger towns and cities. Pamela left to go to school in Boston and made the city her home.

The store was filled with more people than Meg expected. She grabbed a cart and moved through the aisles, adding foods she'd need for the week. Meg turned down the pet aisle and saw a cat toy of a ball with a bell inside.

"Oh, Trixie is going to love this." She dropped it into her cart along with cans of cat food.

Meg's phone buzzed with a text. She pulled it from her bag and flipped it over. Brandon sent a photo and a caption underneath that read, "Just came today. That was fast. Check your mail."

Meg tapped the picture and enlarged it. He snapped a picture of a letter that said he was transferred to a new location. Brandon kept his job. Meg, buoyed by his news, finished shopping and quickly paid for her items.

She grabbed a latte from the in-store cafe to make up for the morning flop, feeling like she could indulge a little since she'd likely be working again by next week. She hoped to be transferred to a library in a nearby town not too far from home and where they'd have good lunch options nearby. Meg usually packed her lunch, but enjoyed splurging at least twice a month by having lunch from a restaurant.

When she got outside the store in the parking lot, Meg reveled in the warm weather. Today was a great day to have a picnic on the beach. She'd call Sharon to see if she was busy.

Ciara was always busy with the cafe, but she'd ask her too. Meg popped the small hatch on her trunk and loaded her bags. She slipped into the car, buckled up, and made her way back home.

Meg turned on the main road, and drove past the library, where she noticed the barriers were already up, and she could see packing going on through the large-paned window. Meg would miss the old place, but was glad to be moving on too.

Her stomach fluttered with anticipation of what might be her next adventure in a new location. She drove a few more minutes down the road before stopping at the cluster of mailboxes outside the condominiums. Meg got out of the car and fumbled with the mailbox key. She was anxious to see if letter was here too.

Meg rifled through the pile of envelopes.

"It's here." Her hand trembled with anticipation, but she'd wait to open it.

Meg stuffed the envelope in her purse, got back in the car, then drove to her parking spot in front of the townhome.

Meg carried the bags into house and closed the door before Trixie had a chance to run outside. She pulled the mail from her purse when Trixie came out of her hiding place and rubbed against Meg's leg.

"How's my girl?" Meg sat on the sofa with the letter in her hand. Trixie jumped in her lap and purred while Meg scratched her head.

"We've got some important news. Do you want to hear what it says?" Meg carefully tore the envelope apart, removed the letter and shook it open.

A knock at the door caught her attention. Meg wasn't expecting company, and she didn't order anything. She held onto the letter and went to answer the door.

"Hey Meg!" She beamed and leaned into to hug her.

Sharon wore a wide brim hat, red beach sandals and a pretty yellow dress that competed with her sunny smile. A floral beach tote completed the look.

"That dress looks amazing on you."

Sharon stepped into the house and showcased her outfit with a coordinated turn and step.

"Well, aren't you fancy?" Meg laughed. Sharon gave a pageant wave. Fashion was fun to her and the more colorful the better.

Sharon dropped her bag on the sofa. "What are you doing? Do you want to head to the beach? They're having a concert on the pier."

"You read my mind. I planned to call you and Ciara about a beach day."

"Well, here I am." Sharon parked her hands on thin hips. "I'll wait here while you get your things."

Meg dropped the letter on the table. She'd read it on the way over. She wasn't going to pass up sun, music, and good company on a beautiful Saturday afternoon.

"Sure, have a seat. I just went shopping and need to put my groceries away first, then I'll get ready."

"I'll help. We'll get to the beach faster." Sharon grabbed two bags before Meg could say anything. Meg carried another bag to the kitchen then pulled out a bottle.

"Should I bring some wine?"

Sharon mocked wide eyes and a slack mouth, "I can't believe you're asking me that."

Meg chuckled and slipped the bottle into the beach bag on the sofa. She carried the last bag into the kitchen and sat it on the floor.

It tipped over and a small ball rolled out of it. Meg bought the toy especially for Trixie who swatted at it. She jumped back when the bell inside tinkled. Trixie spent the next few minutes knocking the ball around the kitchen then chasing it with each hit.

"Looks like that toy's a winner," Sharon said, then began sneezing, her allergies getting the best of her.

"We better get going. I forgot you can't tolerate cats for too long." Meg smiled at her fur baby. "That'll keep her busy while I'm out. Let me grab my things and we'll leave."

Soon they were nearly out the door when Meg smacked her head, realizing she left the letter on the counter. She backtracked to the kitchen and dropped the envelope in her beach tote. Sharon looked on, puzzled.

"It's a letter about my job," she told Sharon. "I didn't get a chance to read it."

"You're getting another job?"

"No, Brandon got a letter today stating he would be transferred to another location, and I think I may get transferred too."

"See, I knew you had nothing to worry about. Read it in the car while I'm driving." Sharon said, then leaned down and gave Meg one of her famous bear hugs.

Her arms pinned to her body, Meg huffed out, "Thanks, Sharon." Sharon released her grip and Meg took a breath.

The women walked to the car and tossed their beach bags in the back, then hopped into Sharon's cherry red convertible.

Sharon drove onto Main Street, heading toward the direction of the beach. Meg pulled the letter from her pocket and unfolded it. She scanned the first few lines. Her eyes widened. "Are you kidding me?"

Sharon looked over "What? What does it say?"

* * *

Sharon pulled the car over and turned toward Meg, who was now shaking her head.

"I can't believe this."

"Can I read it?" Sharon removed the letter from Meg's grip.

Dear Ms. Hollis,

The Bluewater Branch of Somerset County Regional libraries will be closing and relocating to provide better service to its patrons. All employees have been informed of the changes. We are working hard to retain employment for all employees while the new library is being constructed.

Currently, we are not able to provide employment to you and will place you on furlough. Please see the following paragraphs for the benefits afforded to you while on furlough…

Sharon pulled Meg into a side hug and searched for the right thing to say to her friend. "You still have a job, and I'm sure they will find a position for you… probably in the next week."

"I hope you're right. My mortgage is due and I'm rebuilding my savings after using it for the down payment. I can't miss a paycheck."

"Don't worry. We'll help you," Sharon said.

"Thank you, Sharon, that means a lot to me."

Sharon released Meg from her hug, then raised her brows. Her finger shot up like a lightning bolt, as if an idea hung at the end of it. "I know what we should do."

"What?"

"We should go directly to the person who has the authority to change things for you."

"I already spoke to Brandon."

"Meg, you give him too much credit. I'm talking about the mayor… Kevin."

"I don't know about that, Sharon. He might be as blustery as Ciara. They are twins you know."

"I know, but he's a reasonable guy and a bit of diplomacy can go a long way. Besides, I think Ciara got the most bluster of the two." They both laughed.

"So, what's the best way to reach him?" Meg asked.

"Hmm, that's a good question. Ciara doesn't like to ask him favors, although that would be the easiest way."

Both sighed. Meg gave Sharon a half smile. "I think that's a great idea and you'd be the best person to ask Ciara."

Sharon scrunched her nose. They both knew the things that ruffled Ciara's feathers and her brother was one of them.

"How about we play a game of rock, paper, scissors and the loser asks Ciara."

"Sharon, that's a child's game."

She shrugged her shoulders. "Got any better ideas?"

"I guess not." Meg said and readied her hand.

Sharon turned toward Meg, "Rock, paper, scissors, shoot!" Both threw out their hand.

A slow grin spread across her face.

5

Meg released her breath and her shoulders relaxed. Meg's rock beat Sharon's scissors.

"I agree with you now. That was a childish game." Sharon moaned.

"Nope, too late. I won and you promised to ask Ciara about Kevin."

Sharon perked up, "You're right and we're going to get you working again, sooner than later." She said.

Sharon turned the car back on the road. The closer they drove to the beach, the louder the band played. It had been a while since they'd had live music on the waterfront. Sharon tapped her finger on the car wheel to the beat. She was glad to be out on such a glorious day.

Sharon spent most Saturdays tending to guests at The Bluewater Inn. It had been a dream of hers since she was a little girl to own a bed-and-breakfast. In fact, she always knew which one she'd run and how she'd run it. Sharon passed the old Victorian beauty every day on her way to school and dreamed of living there and entertaining endless guests. In college, she jump started her dream by majoring in hotel management.

Sharon worked for years in one of the largest hotel chains in the world. It was the best preparation for what she faced when dealing with guests of the Inn. Her goal was to make sure each visitor ended their stay satisfied. On some days it seemed like an impossible task. So, today was a way to treat herself for a week of particularly thorny guests .

Sharon pulled into the first parking space she could find. The pier was filled with locals and tourists reclined on beach chairs and sitting on blankets.

She loved this town and didn't want to be anywhere else. Sharon put the car in park and popped her trunk.

"I've got chairs for us in the back and packed a few sandwiches in the cooler."

"Thanks, Sharon. You think of everything. What about Ciara?"

"She texted back and is going to try to meet us later on. It's the half-plate special tonight and the restaurant is full."

"I suspected she'd be busy. If she can't make it, we should stop through The Blue Lobster later."

"Sounds like a plan."

Meg and Sharon swung a chair each over their shoulder, and Sharon carried the totes filled with her specialty sandwiches and treats normally reserved for the guests. She whipped up a batch of her famous strawberry lemonade too and thought it might mix well with Meg's wine.

They hustled to find a space as close to the band as possible. The music was going strong, led by a woman with a deep, soulful voice.

"Let's sit here." Meg stopped midway in the crowd. She managed to find a spot big enough to set up the chairs. "We have a good view from here," she said.

"We do. I should have brought the blanket from the car. The wind off the water will make it chilly soon."

"You're right. Give me the keys and I'll go back and get them. Where are they?"

Sharon pulled the keys from the mini pouch that hung in the beach tote and tossed them to Meg.

"In the trunk, you may have to move some things around to find them."

"Okay. Be back soon."

Sharon opened up the chairs and settled in to enjoy their surroundings. She took in a breath of the salty air and closed her eyes. It felt good to be sitting here with nothing to do but enjoy the moment. She scanned the crowd to see if any of her guests from the Inn had come to the concert like she encouraged them to do.

Sharon spotted the mayor not far from her. Meg hadn't returned and this would be a good time for her to chat him up and see what he could do for her friend. If all went well, she wouldn't have to ask Ciara for her help.

Sharon left her chair and walked toward where he sat. The mayor was chatting with someone she didn't recognize.

Kevin resembled his sister in the best ways. His tapered haircut turned his red curls into deep waves that crowned his freckled and bearded boyish face. Hazel green flecked eyes were an additional nod to his Irish roots. Kevin was a charismatic low key power player who many women found hard to resist.

Sharon scooted past layers of concert goers only to watch him get up and leave. She groaned, but kept moving in that direction. She'd introduce herself to the guy the mayor had been talking to and perhaps see where he was staying and drum up some business for the Inn. Sharon reached the man's side and stuck out her hand.

"Hello, my name is Sharon Stewart. I'm the owner of The Bluewater Inn on the east side of Bluewater Shores."

The man looked up, smiled back, and shook her hand. "Nice to meet you, Sharon, my name's Chase."

"Are you a friend of the mayor?" she asked.

Chase nodded his head "More like a consultant."

"Really?" Sharon gestured to the spot next to him and turned to see if Meg returned. She hadn't. "Do you mind if I sit here?"

Chase moved a small bag to make some room for her. "Sure." Sharon sat in space he made. He seemed friendly enough and open to chat.

"How do you like our town?"

"I like it a lot and hope to buy something in a year or so." He glanced in the direction that the mayor had gone.

"It's a great town and location, especially if you like quiet winters. The town tends to slow down during that time. The tourists leave and it's just the locals. Do you plan on becoming a part-time resident?"

"Uh, I'm not sure. It depends on how the development goes?"

Sharon gave him a sharp look. "Development? Are you part of that dreadful plan?"

Chase frowned and leaned away. "Well, in fact, I am. My company has drafted a schema for the waterfront and parts of Main Street. I promise it's not a dreadful plan and is just what this sleepy town needs to save it from itself." He explained politely.

Sharon pursed her lips to hold on to her diplomacy. "I think our sleepy town is fine just the way it is."

Chase raised his brows, smirked then looked forward. "You see this old pier we're sitting on"—he gestured in a sweeping motion—"it's really not ideal for having a concert like today. Folks could have a better experience with the new design. We have seating and open space too. The band or whatever entertainment there would be will have an elevated stage. The plans are magnificent. I can't wait for the town to see them."

Sharon's jaw tightened. "What makes you think the town is interested in your plans?"

"Who wouldn't want to see something new and better?"

"Me, for one." Her smile slipped to a forced grin.

Chase scratched his neck, then looked around. "I'm not sure how long your mayor is going to be. He had to take a call. I can tell him you stopped by."

Sharon could see Meg walking back to their chairs and stood up.

"No, don't worry about it. I'll catch up with him later. Nice meeting you, Chase."

He stood up and offered his hand. Sharon shook it, then walked back to her chair.

"Hey, where did you go?" Meg asked.

Sharon plopped down in her chair and blew out an exasperated breath. "I just had the most annoying conversation with someone."

"I could tell something was bothering you. What happened?"

"Well, it's more like who happened."

Meg scooted her chair closer to Sharon. "Okay, who did it?"

Sharon took in a breath and began. "I saw the mayor sitting not far from us and thought it would be a good time to plug your job and to chat about the library closing. The problem was he left his chair before I could get to him and so I chatted with his guest instead."

"Who was the guest?" Meg leaned in.

"His name was Chase, and he described himself as the mayor's consultant."

"Consultant? What kind of consultant?"

"Exactly what I thought. So, we continue talking and as it turns out, he's the developer who's put together a plan to change Bluewater, including the pier we're sitting on right now."

"You're kidding! He showed you the plans?"

"Not exactly, he described the *new and improved pier* and said the current one wasn't good enough. Oh and get this… he wants so save our town."

Meg wrinkled her nose. "Oh, he's got nerve. I'm sure if he's talking like that to the mayor, then that development plan won't last long. We love our pier and town just the way it is and it doesn't need saving."

Sharon put on her sunglasses and reclined in the chair. "I'm sure you're right, Meg. I hope the mayor knows the town folks well enough to send this guy packing."

Meg caught a glimpse over Sharon's head. "Hey, there he goes."

"Who?" Sharon sat up and took off her glasses.

"The mayor. I'm going to go over there and tell him what I think about all of this."

"Meg, don't bother. Let's enjoy the concert. We have plenty of time to talk to him."

Meg sat back in her chair and pressed her lips together. Sharon glanced at her friend.

"Go ahead, Meg, but don't say I didn't tell you."

"I know what I'm doing. Be right back."

6

Meg stopped beside the mayor who was still chatting. He paused to turn toward her, and she noticed his eyes took a special interest, almost a sparkle. The other people paid them no mind and continued their conversation.

"Hi, Meg. How've you been?"

"Hello Mayor Kevin, I wish I could say good, but things aren't going so well."

"Really? Anything I can help you with?" He flashed a warm smile. Kevin seemed genuine. Maybe he could help her.

Meg smiled back and crossed her arms. "I'm sure you know about the library closing and the plans to build a new one."

Kevin held one arm across his body and rested the other one on it while stroking his beard. "Yes, I know about it. From what I've seen, it'll bring better services to the people who visit it. Have you seen the plans?"

"No, I haven't seen the plans, but my point is, when the library closed some of the staff were furloughed and I was one of them. I don't know who else lost their job, but I'm sure they were just as surprised as me, and like me, weren't prepared for the sudden change in their employment status."

He continued to rub his beard, looking thoughtful. "I see what you're saying and didn't know this was an issue. I'll talk to my team and will see what's going on. I want progress to happen in our town, but not at the expense of our citizens losing their livelihood. Thanks for bringing this to my attention."

Meg relaxed her arms. "You're welcome, Mayor."

"Please call me Kevin. We've known each other since middle school, but I can't say I was the nicest of guys back then."

Meg wasn't prepared to reminisce on her middle school days even though he was just awful to her. "Oh, you do remember?"

Kevin's face blushed, which made his freckles fade for that moment. "Yes, I remember, but look at me now, I've done well, don't you think?" he said with playful posing.

"Well, that remains to be seen. Meg poked at him.

"Ouch," he said with a good-natured laugh. Kevin extended his hand and Meg shook it. "Thanks, Meg. I'll find out more about the closing. Plan to call my office next week to follow up."

"I will do that, Mayor… I mean, Kevin." Meg walked away with a light-hearted feeling. Would he really help her? She was hopeful, but cautious since he was a politician.

"Jeez, Meg. He is a politician," she chided herself. Meg's lightness became a little heavier. She thought about Kevin's charm. Her intentions were to be assertive and remain firm about her case and those of her colleagues, but that didn't happen. Instead, she walked away giddy that he remembered her from middle school.

Meg navigated around the packs of concert goers back to her chair where Sharon sat nibbling on on a sandwich.

"So, how did it go?"

"I'm not sure. I didn't know how charming he was, though it seems like he might be able to help. Kevin said to call his office next week."

"So, you're calling him Kevin now?"

"I know, that's weird, isn't it? I started out with Mayor Kevin. He reminded me of our past and before I knew it, I agreed to call him Kevin then said I'd call him at his office next week. Was I completely beguiled, or what?"

"No, not completely. I think he's a nice guy who talked to a nice girl and maybe he'll help."

"Aww, Sharon, be honest."

Sharon took a bite of her sandwich then stared at Meg. "Honestly, you were duped, bamboozled, beguiled, fooled—."

Meg put up her hand. "Okay, okay I get it."

"So, Are you going to call him next week?

7

Sharon picked up the cooler and placed it in the convertible. Meg loved to ride in Sharon's car with the top down and her sunglasses on. It made everything seem carefree, even when things were not—like now.

She hopped into the passenger's side and slid on her red framed shades. Even though The Blue Lobster wasn't more than a five-minute drive from the shore, she made sure to buckle up because it was the law and safety came first.

Meg played by the books and did things the right way. So why was this happening to her? She followed the rules. Meg needed to talk to Brandon about her job. He said he'd help and put a good word in, and now that he had his job back, he'd surely be able to help her or talk to the regional office.

The engine roared as Sharon started the car. Fast and sporty, it fit Sharon's personality down to the bright cherry red color. She was full of energy and could find the silver lining on the most dismal situations.

Soon they were pulling up in front of The Blue Lobster Grill. The facade was creatively done in pieces of driftwood that had washed up on Bluewater's shores. Ciara commissioned a local artist to create a design that marked it as an authentic seaside restaurant.

Meg pushed through the door to find Ciara chatting with her patrons. Her head was thrown back in a full, throaty laugh followed by a hearty back slap to the unsuspecting man who lurched forward before rubbing his shoulder.

They were shown to their regular spot that always seemed available. It was likely Ciara's table, and the waitstaff knew to avoid sitting people there if possible.

"Hey, when did you two walk in?"

"We just got here and didn't want to interrupt the lively conversation you were having," said Meg.

"Oh, that." Ciara gestured behind her. "We were just talking about all the changes around town and some of the things we ought to do. Did you know they're planning on tearing down the pier and replacing it with some crazy modern metallic clamshell? It's supposedly better for the *acoustics*," Ciara said.

"Sharon heard about that today. In fact, she had a lovely conversation with the developer." Meg turned to Sharon. "What was his name?"

"Chase Stiles. Doesn't that sound pretentious. I bet that's not even his real name. He had some ideas about our town and wasn't very flattering," Sharon said, then picked up her menu.

Meg watched Sharon scan the choices. The menu didn't change and Meg only shook her head, watching Sharon run her finger down the page to only order the same meal each time.

"So, what are you ladies having today, the usual?"

Sharon held up her finger to ask for a moment to choose. Ciara glanced at me and smiled.

"You know I haven't changed my menu in years. How about I get you the shrimp scampi?"

"Thanks, Ciara. You know me so well, and a glass of lemonade too."

Ciara picked up the menus, then turned her attention to Meg for her order.

"I'm not really hungry and that lemonade sounds good. I'll have a glass of that," said Meg.

"All right, I'll be right back." Ciara stacked the menus and handed them to nearby waitstaff.

Meg rested her chin on her hand and sighed. "Do you think we should still ask Ciara to talk with Kevin about my job? I mean, if he heard it from her, then maybe he'd have more motivation to make something happen. And it's not just for me. I'm sure others lost their jobs too."

"I can talk to her like I promised, but we can't count on her talking to Kevin." Sharon shrugged her shoulders. " It wouldn't hurt to ask." She said.

Before Meg could respond, Ciara returned with three full glasses of icy lemonade. An adorable strawberry hung on the side of the glasses. Red and white swirly straws stood in the middle of each glass, making it festive and happy.

"So cute!"

"That looks refreshing." Sharon took one of the glasses from Ciara's tray. Ciara placed a glass in front of Meg, then sat down with the third glass in her hand, placing the tray in the middle of the table. Before they could take a sip, one of the waitstaff dipped in between the group and removed the tray.

"Wow, your staff is amazing." Meg took a sip.

"It's youth. They move around here like lightning and keep the pace of cleaning and serving pretty efficient. I hate to lose them at the end of the summer, but by then the high season is over and the grill slows down."

"What happened to the other young guy who served us a few days ago? The stealthy one?"

"Oh, spiky hair... um." Ciara snapped her fingers trigger her memory.

"You forgot his name?"

"He had a family emergency and needed some time off. He wasn't here long. I'll remember his name later."

Meg took another long sip from her glass. "This lemonade is really tasty. Is it a new recipe?"

Ciara smiled at the compliment. "In fact, it is. I wanted to try something new and added another ingredient to give it a little extra punch."

"Really? What is it?" Sharon's lips puckered around her straw.

"I'd love to tell you, but it's top secret and if I tell you..." They all chimed in, "I'll have to squeeze you." Meg, Sharon, and Ciara launched into full belly laughs. It was a quote from middle school and no one knew who started it, but it stuck with them. They didn't always know when to say it, but knew when it was the right time to say it. It was like they were connected and just knew.

"I guess we better quiet down. We don't want to scare away any of the customers."

Ciara made a final snort and leaned on the table with both arms "I guess you're right, Megs, you've always been the one to straighten us up."

Sharon wiped the tears from her eyes. "That was great, I haven't had a laugh like that in months."

"Me neither. I haven't felt this happy all week."

"Really, Megs? Are you still worried about the job?"

Meg scrunched up her brow. "Things aren't getting better. I got a letter today and my position has been furloughed. Which is the worst position to be in. I have a job, but can't work and can't get paid. I'll file for unemployment, but it won't replace my income. I can't survive long without a full income.

"I see your point, Megs. Is there anything I can do? You're welcome to pick up some hours here. We can use the help during the summer."

"That's really kind of you, Ciara, and I just might take you up on it, but I have another favor to ask."

Sharon cleared her throat and glanced away. Meg ignored her and looked at Ciara.

"I saw Kevin on the pier today and we had a chat about the library closing and the job losses. He seemed genuinely interested in helping me, but I couldn't help wonder if he was just being a politician. Would you mind talking to him so he'll be motivated… knowing we're friends?"

Ciara clasped her hands beneath her chin, then nibbled on her lip. "You know I'd love to help you, but Kev and I are not exactly on speaking terms. I mean we're cordial enough at family functions, but he's not my favorite person right now and honestly, you're better off without a word from me… sorry, Megs." Ciara shrugged her shoulders and gave a half smile to her friend.

"That's fine. I'm sorry to hear you two are not talking."

Sharon cleared her throat again while finishing the rest of her lemonade. Meg looked her way.

"Well, I can check in with Brandon. He said he'd put in a good word and may have some clout since he got his position back so quickly."

"I think that might be a better idea," said Ciara.

"I agree with Ciara. After all, he said he'd help you."

Meg wrapped her hand around the half empty glass of lemonade. The ice began to melt, making the drink less sweet, but she couldn't help herself from drinking it. The secret ingredient was doing it's job. She sipped until Sharon's food arrived. She asked the staff for several small plates.

"Who'd like to share?" Sharon asked.

"I'll have a little." Meg picked up a fork and swirled some

of the fettuccine around until it formed a solid ball around the prongs. She shook it out onto her small plate, then picked a few shrimp from Sharon's plate and plopped them on top.

Sharon pushed the plate to Ciara. Ciara held up her hand. "Thanks, but I've been around food all day. Enjoy your meal."

"Yes, I do understand." Sharon said.

The cafe door opened and a small crowd entered.

Ciara's head perked up in that direction. "It looks like you'll have your chance sooner than later."

Meg turned to see what Ciara was talking about. Brandon and a group of people were just walking into the dining room. He had spotted them and was already a few feet away from the table.

"What's up, Meg?"

* * *

BRANDON PICKED up a chair from a nearby table and tucked it between Meg and Sharon. He sat in the chair and kissed Meg. Ciara grimaced.

"Hey, babe. Hi Sharon." He nodded in Ciara's direction. "Ciara."

"Hey, Brandon," said Meg. She noticed his hair was cut and styled differently then realized it covered most of his forehead. She wanted to apologize to him again for Trixie's sneak attack.

Sharon smiled and waved at Brandon. Her mouth was full of pasta.

"Is that a new cut?" Ciara said. Brandon patted the hair that swooped across his forehead clearly ignoring Ciara's observation.

"So, what are you ladies up to? I thought you'd be out on the pier enjoying the live music. There's a pretty big scene out there."

"We were out there, but decided to come here for something cool to drink." Meg picked up her mostly empty glass of lemonade and shook it."

"That looks good. Do you think I can get one of those too?"

Meg looked at Ciara and could see her jaw flex.

"Sure. I'll be back. Sharon, would you like another?"

"Yes, please."

Ciara left the table and headed toward the kitchen. The same group of customers caught her attention, and she talked with them for a moment before continuing to the back of the restaurant.

"Man, she really hates me. Did I do something to her?"

"No, she's probably having a bad day," said Meg.

"She seems to always be having a bad day when I see her."

Meg patted Brandon on his arm. "Don't worry about it, she'll be fine."

Sharon put her fork down and stared at Meg with an encouraging look. Meg shifted in her seat, then clasped her hands together while resting them on the table.

"Hey, Brandon, did you get more information about starting work?"

Brandon leaned back into the chair. "Nothing more since the letter, and the letter was pretty vague," he said without elaboration.

"What did the letter say, exactly?" Sharon asked, and Meg shot her a look.

Brandon crossed his arms then shrugged. His t-shirt hitched at the shoulders, showing tan lines. "Nothing much, just that my position was transferred, but didn't mention where."

"I guess that makes sense," Meg said, convinced of his honesty. "Did I tell you they furloughed me?"

Brandon uncrossed his arms and leaned on the table toward Meg. "When did you find out?"

"The same day you told me to check my mailbox because you got your letter. So, I thought you could put in a good word for me since you're a supervisor or talk to the district boss or something. Maybe I could get a job where they'll be placing you."

Brandon bit his lip, then looked down at his watch. "I could try," He said half-heartedly. Meg didn't understand his lack of concern.

Ciara returned with the drinks, placed them on the table, and sat down. Sharon took her straw from the drink she just finished and put it into the new glass. "So, you can't help like you promised?"

"Sure. I'll say something, but I can't guarantee a job right away. Besides, you have your job, it's just a furlough."

"Yes, but I need a job that actually pays and not in theory. I've got a new mortgage, remember?"

Brandon looked away blankly. His bold promises from earlier were replaced by a weak offer of support. Meg turned her head to hide the disappointment. She wanted to defend him, but it was hard to do, especially in front of her friends who already had little confidence in him.

"I understand. I'm sure a bunch of other people are asking you for similar favors." Meg said.

She felt Sharon's and Ciara's eyes on her. Brandon must have felt the same as a grin creeped across his face. He pulled out his phone and seemed to be reading a text. Brandon stood up. The tall glass of lemonade sat in front of him, untouched.

"Thank you, ladies, for the lemonade, but I've gotta make an appointment."

"But you didn't even touch the lemonade I brought out for you—that you requested."

Brandon picked up the glass, took a deep sip, and plopped the half-finished glass back down on the table. Ciara's lips curled then puckered as if holding back some choice words.

He smacked his lips and looked at Ciara. "That was better than I thought."

He took out his wallet and placed a few dollars on the table.

"Keep your money. It's on the house." Ciara waved him off.

Brandon picked up the dollars, folded them over each other and slid them back in his pocket.

"Thanks, Ciara. You should keep those on the menu year round. It's the best drink I've had in here."

Ciara rolled her eyes. "I appreciate your input Brandon. Did you say you had somewhere to go?"

"Yes, I'm a busy man with things to do."

"Will you let me know what the district manager says?" Meg asked.

"Sure thing," he said and gave a thumbs-up, then wiggled out of the space he made between Meg and Sharon."

Sharon stirred her drink with the straw. "I'm sure he'll do the best he can for you."

Meg sighed. "Right, and if not, he has a lot of other things to worry about than trying to get my job back."

Sharon and Ciara scooted closer to Meg, then draped their arms over her shoulders.

"You know we'll always be here for you."

"I know you will." Meg said then picked the strawberry off the side of Brandon's glass and chomped into it.

Meg was frustrated with herself. She shouldn't have bought the town house. As always, when her life seemed to be stabilizing she got a swift reminder about the foolishness in putting down roots.

Laughter erupted from the same table Ciara had chatted with earlier.

"So what was all of the hoopla over there with that table?"

"On your way to get the drinks you started another party over there," said Sharon.

Ciara's chair creaked as she rocked in it. A wide grin spread across her face. "Well, we were just talking about what's going on and tossing around some ideas. Not too many of us in town are keen on the proposed changes."

"I don't think many of us are, but it might be good for business. I'd welcome a boost in my income," said Sharon.

"So, that would be a benefit, but how many times have we seen the promise of a little bit of change and then before you know it we're knee deep in commercialization. Bye-bye, small-town stores, hello big box stores, and not to mention what the traffic will be like on our roads."

"You've got a point," said Sharon.

"Well, that may be a problem, but my concern right now is getting my job back so I can keep a roof over my head."

"You can always stay at the Inn with me," Sharon offered.

"Thanks, Sharon, and I know you mean it, but there's nothing like having your own place. You two don't know this, but my mom, sister, and I spent my childhood not knowing where we'd be living next, moving around from town to town, until landing here in Bluewater. It was the first time I'd had any semblance of stability and I refuse to lose it."

Ciara picked up her glass. "Here's to Bluewater Bay." Sharon and Meg clinked Ciara's raised glass "To Bluewater," they said and each tilted their glass then sipped.

Ciara rested her glass on the table, then gestured for them to lean in closer as she lowered her voice. "Now let me tell you my plan…"

8

Meg covered her mouth in surprise. "He really threatened to take your place and use it as part of the development? Can he do that?"

"In so many words and apparently, it can be done through eminent domain, but I'll need to check into that. I didn't think private developers had that power and assumed it was limited to the government… but that was his threat," said Ciara.

"So, you met Mr. Stiles too. He's such a snake. When did you meet him? Sharon asked.

"The other day. A couple of customers and myself were watching the construction going on at the library and some of the workers were parked in my parking lot. And so naturally, I went over to ask them to move their cars since it's for customers only."

"I'm sure they didn't expect that kind of boldness from anyone in town. Good for you, Ciara!" Said Sharon.

"So, what happened next?"

"Well, I went to find the foreman, but they directed me to

a tall man with slicked hair who introduced himself as Chase."

Sharon and Meg sat enthralled in the story. Both leaned on their hands with elbows on the table. All eyes were focused on her, which appeared to encourage Ciara to tell the most dramatic version she could.

"So, he called you a townie? Oh no." Meg turned to Sharon whose mouth had formed a perfect O along with her widened eyes taking in the details of the story.

"What did you tell him, I'm sure he wasn't prepared for what came next," Sharon said.

"I told him he didn't know who he was messing with and if he knew better that he'd take his fight elsewhere. That's when he said he knew exactly who I was. Kevin's sister, and if I didn't watch it he'd include my grill in the development plans whether I liked it or not."

Ciara's face flushed as if reliving that part of the story. The chair scraped across the floor as she pushed back from the table to give herself room to breathe after the telling.

Meg fanned her friend with a napkin. "I'd be hot too. The nerve of that guy."

"You see how annoyed I'd been at the pier after talking to him," Sharon added.

Ciara's face returned to its normal color. She picked up a napkin and wiped her brow then looked around the cafe. A few of the tables were empty and being bussed by the waitstaff.

"Wow, Ciara, so what are you going to do now?"

"Like I said earlier, I have a plan to put Mr. Stiles in his place."

Sharon's plate was now empty as well as two glasses. "Really, like what?"

Meg didn't know Sharon's secret for staying thin since she never left a plate empty. She pushed Brandon's half empty glass toward the center of the table where it was swiftly bussed away.

"You'll have to come by the place on Monday and see."

"You just can't tell us?" asked Sharon

"Nope, just come by for lunch. No, make that dinnertime."

Meg shook her head. "I may not be able to make it. I have an appointment at four o'clock and I'm not sure how long it'll be."

"That's not a problem. Come by anytime this week. You won't miss it."

Ciara smiled triumphantly, like the deed was done. Meg could only guess what her dear friend had in mind. She was sure it was bold, but Meg's thoughts were elsewhere. She not only received the furlough letter, but her last paycheck hit her account yesterday. Meg needed to make hard choices, and Brandon's lukewarm response to her request for help made things less hopeful. Meg felt her anxiety rise. She took a deep breath. "Well, ladies, I have to get going; I'm sure Trixie is waiting by the door for me."

"Wait, don't you want a ride? I know you don't live that far, but…"

"Thanks, Sharon, but I could use the walk. If you don't mind, could you bring the things I left in your car tomorrow or even Monday?"

"Sure, I can drive by tomorrow afternoon."

Meg stood and pushed the chair to the table. "Talk to you ladies later," she said and waved before heading out of the cafe.

Lively music drifted from the beach. Pockets of people walked along Main Street, stopping to peek into local shops or read posted menus on restaurant windows. Soon the dinner crowd would fill the cafes and seaside eateries.

Usually, Meg enjoyed the energy from the Saturday night activities, but not tonight.

She hung her purse across her body and strolled in the direction of her townhome, away from the beach scene. Thoughts from dinner with Sharon and Meg kept her company while she walked.

Brandon's face popped in her mind and Meg's anxiety began to rise again. She picked up the pace and was at the door to her place twenty minutes later. The walk had done her some good. She liked where she lived and her life here in Bluewater.

Meg wasn't sure how things would turn out, but decided she would do what was necessary to keep it.

* * *

MEG OPENED the door and as she predicted Trixie sat there waving her tail back and forth questioning her time gone.

"Oh, Trixie. I was hanging out with some friends. You know Sharon can't come here because she's allergic to you, so we went to the pier to hear some live music."

Meg crouched and held out her hand. Trixie trotted over and purred while Meg rubbed her calico head. All was forgiven.

She stood and hung her purse on the hook beside the door and walked into the kitchen to pour herself a glass of water.

Trixie followed behind her, knowing what was coming. Meg reached into the cabinet and sprinkled a few treats in her hand, which got Trixie's attention. She then pawed at Meg's legs. Meg bent down and allowed Trixie to nibble at the treats from her palm while she rubbed her head.

"Now, that's a good girl. Sorry to have been gone so long,

but you were fine." Trixie ate the last treat then followed Meg into the living room and hopped on the sofa beside her.

Meg took out her phone and navigated to her banking app.

"What are we going to do, girl? Today was my last pay day until I start working again. I have little in savings and we'll need this money to live on. I'm sure I'll be working by the end of the month."

Trixie purred in agreement.

"The mortgage is due, but I have a grace period. So, I'll put it all into savings, but will need to come up with another plan to bring in money until this furlough is over. That's a good plan, right, Trixie?" Trixie nestled under Meg's hand as she stroked her belly.

Meg twisted her lips in thought. What did people do when they needed money?

"Aha! I'm going to sell my car. It's not like I need it right now and could save on gas and insurance too."

Meg went online to a car selling website to check out the sale prices of cars like hers. The prices ranged from a little over five thousand to seven thousand dollars. She kept the car in fair condition and could surely get at least six thousand for it.

Next, she searched for the bank that held the loan to her car and tapped on their website. They were closed now, but offered twenty-four-hour customer service. She clicked on the phone icon and a woman with a cheerful demeanor picked up.

"Hello. Thank you for calling Provincial Bank; this is Tina. How may I help you?"

Meg paused. She wasn't sure how to start the conversation about selling her car, and didn't know if they could help her.

"Hi, My name is Meg Hollis and I have a car loan with

your bank. I plan to sell my car and wanted to know the loan balance.

"Hi, Meg, thank you for calling Provincial. I can certainly help you with that. Can I have your account number?"

Meg recited a series of numbers to Tina and waited for the answer.

"It says here, as of today, you owe $9,851.32." Meg's mouth dropped open.

"Are you sure?"

"Yes, that's what it says here on your account, but you're welcome to call back on Monday and speak to a loan representative for the bank."

"Okay, I may do that. Thank you for your help." Meg clicked off the phone, then reached for Trixie and gave her a gentle hug.

"Well, I guess we have to think of another plan. I wasn't expecting to owe that much more money… and how does that happen? Meg put Trixie down and exhaled. She was determined to make things work and was beginning to think that the only person who could help her was the one she would be seeing on Monday.

Meg hadn't visited her mom for months, but she had recently texted and asked her over for an early dinner. Meg and her mom got along for the most part, it was her mother's husband that kept Meg away. She didn't like the way he spoke to Lucille and told him so. He thought Meg was out of place and they haven't spoken since. Meg refused to visit her mom while Allan was home. But now she was invited to dinner with them both.

Meg sighed. She went to the door and slipped on her shoes. "I'll be right back, Trixie." Meg opened the door and headed to the mailbox. She checked the mail earlier today, but thought letters might have crossed. Perhaps, by some chance, a letter with her reassignment, like Brandon's had been delivered, and she missed it.

Her mailbox was centered in the collection of mini steel doors. She unlocked the box and the small door creaked open. Meg stuck her hand into the deep rectangular vestibule and felt around. Nothing. She pulled her hand out, relocked it, and moaned. Meg fought off the creeping despair and took several deep breaths. Tomorrow was Sunday, and the weather called for warm weather and sunshine.

She'd make a dent in her book list by reading on the beach. Meg wanted a day to escape from her mounting issues.

Sunday would be her day. The day before she promised to have dinner with with her mom and Allan.

She'd have to prepare for a meal with the colonel. Meg rarely left with her nerves intact. His requests were veiled orders and Meg worried if her mom was truly happy.

If she was honest, Meg wasn't up for dinner with the colonel, but didn't have a good reason to cancel. Should she lie?

9

*G*reen had always looked good on Meg. She twirled in the mirror to see herself from the rear. Somehow, today, it didn't seem to be working and she thought the same about her mother's marriage to Allan.

He was a nice guy and generous. He'd been married once and had a daughter who lived in New York. Allan was a soldier who spent his life defending our country and moved ambitiously the through the military.

Lucille, who'd never had anyone care for her in the way Allan did, was immediately smitten. So, when he popped the question, Lucille said yes without hesitation. Meg was happy for her mom until they began having regular dinners.

Allan had not left his military ways behind and ordered mom around like she was his subordinate. Meg watched her mom become less of the vibrant, carefree spirit to a timidity unlike she'd seen. It hurt Meg to see this happen, and when she could tolerate it no more, she spoke up. That was months ago, and she had been banned from the Carson compound, as Meg liked to call it.

Mom reached out recently and Meg ached to see her. So

she agreed to meet with Lucille, but with a catch... Allan would be there. Up until her mom's wedding, Meg and Mom would have sporadic lunches in town or she'd drop by when Allan was away on business. Meg should've known that wouldn't last long since her mom began to complain about sneaking to see her youngest daughter and wanting family to come over as the holidays approached.

Meg changed into a pale yellow dress that was just as flattering and made her feel happy. She scrunched her damp hair and allowed it to air dry. Trixie stretched her body along the bedroom's window sill to catch the sun's fading rays. Meg ran her hands over the small burrs that clung to her belly and carefully plucked them off.

"Trixie, if you don't stop playing in that burr patch you won't be going outside, and we know how much you enjoy your outside time."

Trixie purred as Meg removed the last burr and patted her belly. "We'll brush you later and check to make sure your treatment is working."

Meg didn't really worry about Trixie going outside during the day. It was a safe place and she always came back. She avoided letting her out at dusk and the early morning since those were dangerous times. The Cape was home to coyotes and they were most active during those hours.

Meg checked herself one more time, then packed a small purse and was careful to add a couple of aspirin for the headache she'd get after dealing with Allan.

She walked out the door and got into her trusty Honda. The sporty two door screamed her name when she saw it on the lot three years ago. It was the first time she'd bought a car on her own and had been happy with it until recently. Learning she'd been upside down on the loan changed her plans. She drove over to Lucille and Allan's thinking of ways to ask for a loan. It wouldn't be easy, but she'd talk to her mom when Allan wasn't around.

The Carsons lived on multi acreage land. It was a grand home with large windows framed by columns that lined a wide porch. The entrance led to a circular driveway that held Allan's small fleet of cars. He preferred to drive around town in his black BMW, but drove the large tank-like SUV on his trips out of town. Meg was never sure about which war he left town to fight.

His trips weren't her concern and he made that clear. Meg swore his business was espionage, but Lucille didn't find her theories amusing. Not only had Lucille become a soldier, but she lost her sense of humor too.

Meg pulled up next to her mom's sedan. She put the car in park and looked skyward.

"Please let this be the quickest dinner possible and... with chocolate cake." Meg opened the door and swung both feet to the ground. She reached for her purse, hooked it on her shoulder then stood up taking a deep breath. Meg willed one foot in front of the other and marched toward the front door.

Lucille flung the door open as soon as Meg's foot hit the first step. Her mother's face was genuinely happy. Meg's pretty face mirrored Lucille's. Her naturally pink lips pouted to a cupid's bow and handsomely matched a dimpled chin. Lucille wore a short bob that played up the single gray patch at the front, making it look intentional and sophisticated. She was flawlessly elegant.

They hugged, then Mom pecked her on the cheek and rubbed the spot like she always did.

"To make it stick," she said.

"Mom, I'm not a little girl anymore."

"I know, but you'll always be my little girl. That yellow

dress looks wonderful on you. I haven't seen you wear it before. Is it new?"

"No, not really. I bought it a few months ago, but haven't had an occasion to wear it." Meg splayed her hands and patted the stiff folds in front of the dress."

"Well, I like it. Come in, Allan is in the office talking to a client. He'll join us soon."

"Not if he's making a trades deal with a foreign entity, " Meg said with a single raised eyebrow and a chuckle.

"Shush Meg! He'll hear you."Lucille gestured for Meg to enter. "Come in."

The large open foyer led to several rooms that circled the space. It was immaculate with Lucille's decorative touches guided by the help of a hired designer. Meg always thought it was too much house for two people, but Lucille fell in love with the house and Allan bought it for his new bride.

Mom wanted to raise Meg and her sister in a home like this, but instead, they moved from place to place. Sometimes an apartment and other times with family until Mom could find a place to live. Lucille was an artist, a dancer, and found work where she could at different studios or with short gigs in productions. They ultimately landed in Bluewater when Lucille met and fell in love with a man who worked for the Cape Cod Air Force Station. When that didn't work out, she met Allan.

Meg followed her through the space into the family room, adjacent to the oversized gourmet kitchen.

Lucille grabbed Meg's hand and pulled her toward the patio doors. "Dinner will be ready shortly. Let's sit by the pool until then."

The smell of citrus clued Meg into the dinner. It was her favorite and the one Mom loved to make the most.

"Herbed lemon chicken?"

"You can tell?" Lucille smiled.

"Yes, thank you, Mom."

The two settled into the mahogany brown wicker chairs with floral cushions near the shaded end of the pool. Meg's back faced the house, giving her a view of the pool and attached hot tub. A pinstripe umbrella covered the table and was a complement to the fabric on the chairs. She enjoyed time spent with her mom. Through high school and afterwards their relationship had been strained and even broken before Meg left town. But they were in a good place now.

"Oh Meg, I should have brought out something for us to drink. What would you like, sweetheart?"

"Water is fine. Have you spoken to Pamela? "

"Not recently, I know she's busy with your nephew. His birthday is coming up soon."

"I can't believe another year has gone by. I'll have to remember to send a card and gift."

"How are you? How's your new home?" Lucille asked.

"Well, things are a little crazy now, but they should be back to normal soon."

"What do you mean?"

"I don't know if you've been in town, but the library closed and I was furloughed."

"Oh no, are you okay?"

"I'm hoping to hear back soon about going back to work, but to be honest, it's a little scary."

Lucille's face contorted with concern. "Do you need any help?"

Meg dropped her hands into her lap and picked at her nail, avoiding eye contact with her mom.

"Um, I was hoping to borrow some cash until I went back to work."

"You know I'll do what I can, but Allan will have to approve it."

Meg sighed. She knew the money she wanted to borrow was not Mom's. Allan paid for everything.

"I know, but we don't have the best relationship, and I was hoping you could talk with him."

Lucille clasped her hands together. "You may have to apologize to him."

Meg stiffened. "But, I didn't do anything wrong. It wasn't right for him to talk to you like that."

"I know you don't like his demeanor, but that's his personality."

"He's a bully."

"Meg, that's not fair," Lucille said. "Look, I'll get our drinks and we'll talk some more, but I think you need to prepare yourself to apologize. That is, if you want the money."

Lucille pushed her chair away from the table and moved to stand. Meg blew out a short breath. Lucille could be blunt when she wanted which gave Meg hope that her mom wasn't a complete pushover to Allan.

The patio doors closed and heavy footsteps approached from behind. Lucille's eyes darted past Meg's shoulders. She stood fully and tucked a lock of hair behind her ear.

"Hello, dear. Meg's here, and I was about to get us some drinks until dinner was done."

"I'll have a gin and tonic," he snipped.

Broad shoulders dressed in a navy polo rounded the table and sat across from Meg.

"How are you, Megan? It's been a while."

Meg and Allan's last interaction did not go well, to say the least. She didn't know what to expect today, but assumed she'd have her mother as a buffer while she was there.

Lucille turned to Meg. "Did you want ice too?" Meg nodded and watched he mom head back to the patio doors.

Now it was just her and the general. Her stomach churned. He seemed bigger than the last time she saw him.

"I'm great, Allan. How're things with you?"

* * *

"I'M NEVER DOING THAT AGAIN." Meg chided herself.

Safe in the car, Meg rested her head on the steering wheel. Dinner lasted far too long, and Allan was just as impossible as ever. He ordered Lucille around like a little soldier, and she seemed content to comply.

Was she blind? Is this what love does to you. Meg would never allow Brandon to fool or mistreat her. She took out an aspirin, crunched it between her teeth and attempted to swallow the chalky jagged pieces. Of course she gagged and nearly choked. A few hard swallows saved her from having to run back into the flames of the Carson Hell.

Lucille hinted at an apology to Allan, but Meg felt even more certain it would never happen. She stuck the key into the ignition and started the car. Meg backed out of the space into the circular driveway. She was glad to on her way out of Allan's compound.

She took the long route home and drove through town. Meg was curious about Ciara's surprise. It was past dinnertime. Ciara promised to reveal it by then to her and Sharon. Although Lucille served chocolate cake for dessert, Meg's appetite evaporated halfway through dinner and she couldn't enjoy the rest of Lucille's meal. Now a safe distance away, her appetite returned. She felt guilty about not eating her mother's food, but torture and dining were not a suitable mix.

She'd stop in for the surprise and some of Ciara's famous strawberry shortcake. Meg's mouth watered at the thought of a biscuit filled with heavy whipped cream and marinated strawberries. The rustic recipe remained a favorite through the summer season.

Meg turned the corner onto Main Street. A small crowd was gathered outside of The Blue Lobster. She drove past the restaurant and pulled into an off street parking lot. Meg checked her face, got out of the car, and walked to the front of the building. She stood outside the crowd, surprised at the line to get in. Meg looked past the crowd and up to the window where people were pointing. This was Ciara's big surprise.

10

*C*iara planted her hands on her hips. A wry smile formed as she watched the crowd in front. She had succeeded in bringing attention to her cause… "Save Bluewater from Big Business," said the banner spread across her windows.

The conversations with her friends confirmed that she couldn't sit around and allow a big time developer to come in and turn the lives of her friends, family, and customers upside down. Meg had been the first casualty, and some of her patrons expressed their dissatisfaction with watching the library being demolished. What many of them didn't know is that there was more to come.

The front door opened, bringing in a gush of cool salt air and Meg.

"Hey, what's up, Megs?"

"I see your surprise is causing a stir out there."

"Isn't it great! That'll show Chase Stiles that he can't boss us around with his fancy plans for our town. We're just not going to stand for it."

Meg wiped the sweat from her brow and looked around

for a seat. One of the servers walked past with a tray appetizers and drinks.

"Can I get a glass of water?" Said Meg.

"Sure. Are you okay?"

"I'll be fine." Ciara led Meg to their usual table and waved over the closest server.

"Would you mind bringing us a pitcher of water and a couple of glasses?" The young woman nodded and hurried off to take another order.

"You had an appointment or something, right?

"If you want to call it that. I went to Lucille's for dinner."

Ciara's eyes widened in surprise. "Really? How is Lucille and…"

"Allan. She's fine and he's still a wad of… well, you know he's still the same."

Ciara laughed. She knew Meg well enough to understand she'd need more than a glass of water after having dinner with Allan and Lucille, but the bar was closed.

"Hey, I wish I could offer you more than a glass of water, but there's lemonade in the kitchen if you want."

Meg shrugged. "Water is fine. I just need a moment to breathe… felt like I was holding my breath the entire time during dinner."

Ciara reached over and gave Meg's hand a reassuring squeeze. "It'll be fine. You had dinner with Allan and your mom, and I'm sure that'll be your good deed for a while."

Meg shook her head." I wish that were true, but I may need to brave another dinner or something."

Ciara smiled, then turned to the commotion just outside her door. Meg looked too, and they both stood to see what was going on, on the usually peaceful Main Street.

A small group of people walked back and forth in front of the library holding signs decrying its closing. Nancy marched in the middle of the group, shouting along with the rest of the protesters half her age. She held a sign in one hand and her cane in the other while chanting, "Save our town!" Ciara always suspected she was a firecracker, but had no idea until now. The others included a mix of Bluewater's residents carrying signs with similar messages.

Meg turned to Ciara and chuckled. "Look what you started."

Ciara's hand covered her mouth to block a smile. She was amused and surprised. Ciara loved this town and its residents, but to see it all in action nearly brought her to tears.

"Are you crying?"

Ciara sniffled and then wiped her eyes. "No, of course not, must be my allergies."

"Your allergies are in the fall, it's only July."

"You know me too well, Megs. Let's go outside and get a closer look."

Ciara led the way as the two walked onto the sidewalk into the crowd that stood in front of The Blue Lobster.

The sheriff's car rolled up in front of the cafe. Sheriff Peter Mendoza got out of his car with a bullhorn and headed across the street to the protesters. He knew every resident and sauntered toward the scene getting ready to seemingly break up the crowd in front of them. "Oh no!" Ciara cried.

The sheriff tugged his pants up over a protruding belly then held the bullhorn to his mouth. "Please disperse from in front of the library or I will cite you all for disorderly conduct."

The picketers ignored the sheriff and shouted louder, "Save our Town."

"Break it up or I'll ticket each and every one of you," he tried again.

This time Nancy shouted back, "We're not wrong, they are!" She pointed her sign toward the developer's banner that hung on the partially demolished building and continued her march. The rest of the marchers shouted in agreement.

Ciara pushed through the crowd on her side of the street to get a closer look. Her heart pumped with excitement, wanting to join her fellow resisters.

"This is my last warning. Leave peacefully from in front of the library now!"

The crowd grumbled with an obvious desire to continue. Ciara waved both hands at the crowd. "Come over here for free coffee," she said gesturing to her placard attached to the wall of the cafe. Several of the protesters including Nancy lowered their picket signs and glowered at the sheriff while making their way over to the grill. Nancy gripped her cane and hammered her way past the sheriff. A loud yelp came from Sheriff Mendoza as he hopped on one foot. Nancy smiled slyly as she stepped on the curb and walked into the restaurant door held by Ciara.

"Ciara, what are you doing?" Meg whispered.

"I have no idea, but we'll see."

Meg shrugged her shoulders and shook her head. "I'm going home and nurse my headache. I'll talk to you later."

"Sure thing." Meg left and the last of the group entered the door.

Ciara directed the small group to sit at two separate tables. She waved a server over. "Sam, take orders for coffee. It's on the house." Ciara positioned herself at the front of both tables and looked over the group who excitedly talked about the protest.

Nancy hung her cane on the back of her chair and peered at Ciara. "So, did you invite us here for coffee or what?"

Ciara held up her hands in defense. "I didn't want to see you nice people get in

trouble with the law."

"Well, with that sign hanging up outside, you don't seem

to be afraid of a little confrontation yourself," someone in the group teased and they all laughed.

The restaurant door opened and closed firmly behind Ciara.

She watched the expressions of her patrons turn from cheer to annoyance. Heavy steps ambled beside her. The sheriff canvassed the space and then Ciara. He tipped his hat at her before addressing the crowd.

"I hope you all are enjoying yourselves and that coffee. If any of you think I'm going to go easy on you the next time you go out there marching about, you thought wrong. And Ms. Nancy, I'm gonna let that assault with your cane slide this time. I've put people older than you behind bars."

The group jeered and hissed at the sheriff. He held up a silencing hand to stop the noise.

"Whose side are you on, Sheriff? This is your town too," a voice piped up.

"Yes, this is my town, but my job is to keep order and uphold the law, which I will do."

The group grumbled.

Ciara crossed her arms, incensed at his threats. She felt his eyes looking down on her and turned to meet his stare. "Now, Ms. McDougal, I have a lot of respect for your family with your brother being the mayor and all, but I can't have you inciting protests with your signs. It's your right to hang it and express yourself, just remember we like civility in our town… and you're a nice woman."

Ciara nodded while heat seared through her. She knew when someone was trying to put her in her place and she didn't like it, to say the least.

"Thank you, Sheriff. This *nice* woman appreciates all you do for our town and if you don't mind me saying, peaceful protesting is civility to which I support."

Cheers sprang up from the group with Nancy waving her

cane, nearly hitting the gentleman beside her. Luckily, he ducked just in time to avoid a possible trip to the ER.

"You tell him, Ciara," Nancy said.

The sheriff's ears turned a bright red and through pressed lips he whispered, "And the last thing you want to do is cause trouble for yourself and this business." Sheriff Mendoza tipped his hat and marched out of the restaurant. Upon his exit, the room erupted.

"You go, Ciara!"

"Way to stand up to a bully!"

"Yes! Ciara for Mayor!"

Ciara waved her hands to calm the group, but couldn't shake the jolt of energy she felt in standing up for the town, but she heard the sheriff's whispered warning.

Was this worth the risk?

11

The creamy sauce bubbled in the pan, sending the aroma of clam chowder into the living room. Meg put down her phone and walked in the kitchen to check on it. It was her comfort food, and she tried to keep a container in her freezer for times like these.

Meg rummaged through the utensil drawer until she found a spoon to stir the chowder, releasing more of the savory scents mixed with kernels of sweet corn. Meg took a whiff and her mouth watered with anticipation. She poured the chowder into a deep bowl and plunked the spoon inside and watched it slowly sink into the thick sauce. Meg needed to add a crunch to meal. She poked around her cabinet and grabbed a box of oyster crackers. Clam chowder was really a comfort cold weather meal, but Meg needed some summer comfort. She carried her meal back to the living content for now.

Trixie tucked herself into her favorite corner of the couch and snored. Who knew that cats could snore so loudly. Meg made a mental note to talk with the veterinarian about it.

She scrolled through her email on the phone between bites of food.

Meg hoped to hear something by now about the job, but nothing yet. Lucille had called while she was in the kitchen, undoubtedly checking on Meg and wanting to know if she'd take the loan.

Meg checked to see if Brandon called. He seemed distant lately. Starting when she asked him to put a good word in for her. It was like he didn't really want to help despite her earlier promises to be there for her. She wondered if someone or something had become more important. Meg hated to be so dependent on him, but he knew so many important people. At least that's he said.

Her stomach rumbled to remind her of the warm bowl of chowder. Chunks of potatoes with clam bits and corn filled the spoon while the thick white sauce clung to all sides of the spoon.

"Mmm, this is so good." Meg dipped the spoon for another bite when the phone rang again. Lucille's number popped up.

"Argh!" Meg cried then pressed the screen to answer.

"Hey Mom. I'm eating. Can I call you back?"

"Hi Honey, I wanted to check on you. Are you home? Do you have a minute to talk?

This was Lucille exerting her mother authority by clearly ignoring Meg's request. It was one of her passive aggressive techniques that drove Meg bonkers. She decided to not fight it tonight.

Sure mom. I'm fine. Just had to get back to the house and let Trixie in before it got too late."

"Oh good. Did you think anymore about taking the loan." She said then paused.

Meg shifted the phone to her other ear. She this was

really why she called. Meg anticipated the next line of questions.

"Yes, I thought about it on the way back home, and I know you think an apology is a simple thing to do to get the money, but the truth is I didn't do anything to apologize for."

Meg sighed, listening to her mom justify Allan's behavior… he was military… his upbringing was hard—*so was mine,* yadda, yadda, yadda.

"Mom, that may be true, but it doesn't give him the right to order you around and talk to you like some subordinate, and from the look of things during dinner he hasn't changed, so no apology from me."

"I think you're being stubborn, Meg," her mom scolded her like she was still a child.

"I'm not being stubborn and I understand no apology, no loan." Trixie stirred and opened her mouth to yawn, curling her petite pink tongue. She stretched her front legs before standing to arch her back. Meg reached over and scratched Trixie's ear while listening to Lucille's defend.

"Hey, Mom, Can we talk about this latter. I gotta go. My food is getting cold."

Meg put the phone down on the table and leaned back onto the sofa. It felt good to reject Allan's conditions for the loan, but it didn't solve her problem. Who could she rely on? Meg checked the clock which read 4:38.

The county offices closed in less than half an hour. Should she call to make an appointment with Mr. Harris? Maybe he could help.

"What do you think, Trixie girl? Should I call now?" Trixie purred, then jumped onto the floor and walked toward the kitchen. "I'll take that as a yes."

Meg scrolled through her address book, then clicked the call icon.

"Somerset County Libraries," said a friendly voice.

"Hello, my name is Megan Hollis and I'm a librarian in the Bluewater Bay Branch. I'd like to make an appointment to see the regional director, Mr. Harris."

The woman who answered the phone offered Meg a date and time that she immediately agreed to take. She didn't have the luxury of choice.

"Yes, tomorrow…I will be there. Thank you so much."

Meg hung up the phone, surprised at how easily that went. It heartened her to think this appointment might help get her job back. Meg picked up the bowl and took a spoonful of the cold and congealed chowder.

"Yuck!" She spat into the napkin then marched to the kitchen and microwaved her meal. There's nothing worse than a cold bowl of chowder… well, except maybe apologizing to Allan.

Meg counted on the meeting with Mr. Harris going well since Brandon seemed preoccupied. If not, she bristled at the idea of making that phone call to the colonel.

12

Meg rose early, showered, and dressed. She didn't want to be late for her appointment with the director. Meg practiced what she would say and even printed off a copy of her résumé, just in case... Just in case there was an opportunity for something unexpected.

Setting up this meeting to get her job back felt assertive and bold. She prepared herself for all possibilities of the meeting, ready to meet the challenge. Meg put the résumé in a folder and tucked it in her tote.

She took a last look in the mirror at the front door, and nodded at her reflection. Almost forgetting her purse, Meg walked back to her bedroom and again headed for the door, but not before she made several trips back to retrieve several more forgotten items. She was procrastinating and knew better. If Meg didn't get going soon her head start would turn into a late arrival.

Meg bent down and scratched Trixie behind the ear. "Wish me luck!"

Trixie gazed up at Meg, uninterested, between licks of her

coat. Meg opened the door, patted her bag to hear her keys jingle and finally walked through the door.

Over the forty minute drive, Meg imagined the worst case scenarios which didn't help. In fact, she arrived in Remington more anxious than the beginning of her trip.

Remington was a small city with big buildings, the seat of county offices. Meg had only been here a handful of times, each time related to something for her job. She liked the city. It wasn't huge like Boston, but big enough to keep life interesting. She could see herself working here.

The building housing the regional offices came into sight. Meg looked around for street parking as she didn't want to have to pay for a garage with her limited funds, presently. After driving for about ten minutes, she knew she would have to put the car in the nearest garage and hoped they would not charge an obscene amount to park there. Meg took the next left into a multi-level garage attached to the offices and found a parking space on the first level.

"This is going to be a good day, and I'm going to get my job back," she whispered to herself.

A quick check in the mirror showed that her lipstick was intact and not a hair out of place. Meg reached for her bag, opened the door, and got out the car, sure of where she was going. Instead of walking through the garage, Meg walked outside to the front of the building.

It was an old red brick building; the kind found throughout New England, built to withstand the climate and mimic what Meg had seen in the United Kingdom.

Meg entered the building and pressed the button for the elevator. When the doors opened she entered, followed by a few other people who were probably on their way to work and not there for the same reason as her. She missed feeling productive.

"Can you press eight please?" she asked a pretty woman

wearing a purple sweater with a mini white flower pattern similar to one she owned. The woman smiled and pressed the button.

"I'm going to that floor too."

Meg said, "I like your sweater."

"Thank you. It's my favorite."

Meg smiled back, but couldn't shake the sense of rivalry that rose in her. She didn't know the woman and the interaction was pleasant.

Meg shook off the feeling. The elevator car reached the eighth floor, and the two women got off. She took a right and the woman followed her. Meg stopped at the receptionist's desk and watched the purple flowered sweater woman walk past straight into the office behind the desk.

"Good morning, I'm here for a meeting with Mr. Harris," said Meg.

"Your name?"

"Megan Hollis."

The receptionist looked down into her book and tapped it with a polished finger. "Yes, I see your name right here. The director will be with you in a minute. He's finishing up a meeting."

"Thank you."

The receptionist gestured toward some chairs to the left. "Please have a seat over there and help yourself to some coffee."

Meg walked over to the coffee machine and poured herself a small cup. Before she took a sip, she checked her bag to make sure she had mints.

Coffee breath during a meeting with the director would make his hair stand on end, but then he didn't have any. She really shouldn't be making jokes about a man who held her future employment in his hands. Meg smiled anyway. She took a sip then sat down holding the cup in two hands. At least her nerves had settled.

"Meg! Is that you?"

Meg looked up to find a familiar face from the regional branch. She couldn't recall her name, but knew she worked the evening hours at the library— well, when there was a library.

"What are you doing here?" asked Meg matching her colleague's level of glee.

"Working. They placed me here after the library closed. I came in with Brandon. He pulled a bunch of us in with him. What are you doing here? Did they place you here too?"

Meg winced. "No, I'm here to meet with the director... hoping to get out of the furlough and go back to work too. It seems like everybody but me is working. I hoped Brandon would have put in a good word as a supervisor, but I'm sure his hands have been full." Meg took a sip of coffee and saw her colleague's eyes flit over Meg's shoulder, then look down.

"More than you know," she whispered.

Meg turned in time to see Brandon walk out of the director's office, grabbing at the hand of the girl with the purple sweater from the elevator. He didn't notice her, and the two of them disappeared behind an office door. Meg's throat tightened. Although she was taken aback by what she saw, it was just a glimpse and could mean nothing at all.

Meg's friendly colleague gestured toward the closed door. "Hey, I'm sure it's nothing," she said.

Meg's eyes shifted away, and she occupied herself by sifting through her bag. "It's okay. It's not like we were serious or anything." Meg pulled out the folder with her résumé inside.

"Miss Hollis, the director will see you now," the receptionist called her.

Meg forced a smile and turned to the girl whose name she

still couldn't remember. "It was great seeing you." She gripped her purse and walked toward the office door.

"Good luck!" she called out as Meg walked through the double doors.

She wanted more than luck. Meg wanted to know who was that woman Brandon followed into the room.

* * *

It was a boxy and unremarkable room. Not what she'd expect of an executive office, but then again everything was in flux. Maybe he'd just moved into the space and didn't have time to fix it up.

A large window brightened the space and offered a breathtaking view of the city's water way. This was the executive view.

"Megan Hollis, right?"

Meg blinked and was back to the moment. "Yes, that's me."

Mr. Harris stood up and came around the conference table that separated him from the rest of the office and extended his hand. Meg shook it with a firm grip, wanting to make a strong impression.

Surprisingly, he stood only a few inches taller than Meg. During the staff meeting, his presence seemed larger, more commanding. Now, the director presented a much more genial persona than he had that fateful night at the library.

"Nice to meet you. I understand you're here to talk about your position in the library." Mr. Harris returned to his chair and flipped through a couple of papers on his desk, tapped on the page and looked up. "I see here you have a position in the Bluewater Branch."

"Yes, I do, but currently the position has been furloughed, and I was here to um…"

Meg's eye caught a glimpse of a pen on the edge of the director's desk. It was a pen that Brandon always used... Navy, ball tipped, the Edge brand with a clip. She'd know it anywhere and didn't see others of the same kind in the holder on Mr. Harris's desk.

Meg's mind flashed to Brandon and the purple sweater girl. Her jaw clenched. "Can I sit down?" she asked.

The director gestured toward the seat next to the pen. She adjusted her gaze.

"Are you okay?" he asked, concern evidenced on his face.

"Yes, I, uh was saying that my position is furloughed and I'm here to talk about it."

Meg's thoughts went from focused to diffused. Maybe she was overreacting and Brandon was goofing around. He hadn't called in a few days and before then seemed distracted.

"Miss Hollis, are you sure there's nothing wrong?"

"Yes, I'm sure... just a little distracted. You have such a beautiful view."

The director turned around as if aware of it for the first time. "Yes, it's pretty nice. Now back to you. So, you worked at the Bluewater Branch under Brandon Lister?"

Meg's stomach tingled "That's right. He's my supervisor."

"Strange he didn't mention you during our staff talks."

Her stomach tightened. "I'm not sure why not, but we were together."

The director's eyebrow slightly lifted.

"No, I mean together... we worked together." Meg corrected herself as heat rose through her cheeks.

The director steepled his fingers and looked down at the paper he'd gazed at earlier.

"Okay. Ms. Hollis, you said that you're here to talk about your position... go ahead," he said and leaned back in his chair.

Meg scooted to the edge of her seat, closer to the desk. She knew exactly what to say.

"I want what everyone else in the building has… a job. I want to come out of furlough and start working again."

He smirked, then folded one hand on top of the other.

"How about I talk to Brandon? We haven't finished staff talks and I'm sure we have more transfers and placements to make. I'll get back to you soon. How does that sound?"

It didn't sound great at all. She came here determined to get her reassignment today and knew she needed to stand firm. Meg straightened her back, then clasped her hands together. "No, how about I call you tomorrow. You and Brandon have had plenty of time to figure out staffing. How does that sound?"

"I-I-I'm sorry… you're going to… what?"

Meg surprised herself, but couldn't undo what she said and frankly promised herself she'd be assertive. But by the look on the director's face, she might have gone too far.

Meg crossed and uncrossed her arms. Maybe she could soften the blow she'd just delivered to her boss's boss. "I can call you tomorrow. You're obviously busy running the department and I can make that my task."

Meg hoped she saved herself from disaster, but only time would tell.

The director stood up, and Meg followed. He extended his hand and gave her another polite handshake. "It was nice meeting you, Ms. Hollis, and I look forward to hearing from you."

"It was a pleasure meeting you too, and we'll talk again tomorrow."

Meg hooked her purse over her shoulder, stuffed the folder back in the tote, then headed out of the large office. She got the feeling the director wasn't expecting Meg's brashness, and to be fair, neither was Meg.

The elevator doors were opening when she walked out of the office, so she rushed to hop on. The quicker she got out of there the better off she'd be. The doors closed behind her, and there was the purple sweater woman. Meg's stomach churned They smiled politely at each other.

"Done for the day?" Meg asked.

"No, work is never done when working with boys, especially when you have to break their hearts. I just want to do my job," she said with a sigh.

"I know what you mean."

But Meg couldn't relate and wanted to know which boy's heart she planned on breaking.

"Are you talking about the guy you were just with?" Meg asked.

13

*M*eg hurried off the elevator and made a beeline through the lobby embarrassed by her futile attempt to connect Brandon with another woman. Did she really expect her to answer the question? Of course the purple flower sweater woman gave her a confused look then hustled off the elevator at the next floor. Meg imagined she thought of her as desperate and prying. It wasn't a good look and Meg hoped to never bump into her again.

Her phone buzzed, but she missed the call. It was from Brandon. She guessed that Mr. Harris called him into his poorly decorated office to talk about her, but it wasn't a good idea to make assumptions. She'd already made a fool of herself twice in the last hour. Regardless, Meg wasn't ready to talk with Mr. Skirt Chaser and stuffed the phone back in her bag.

She pushed through the revolving doors and saw someone wave from the other side. Meg peered through the glass and recognized Mayor Kevin. Meg waved back and continued to push to leave the building. She stepped outside when something tugged at her arm. Meg turned around to Kevin's warm smile and model perfect teeth.

"Hey, Meg, You're leaving?"

Meg shrugged. "I had a short meeting and I'm heading back to Bluewater.

"Oh, I thought maybe you were on your way to lunch."

Meg glanced at her watch. "It's a little early for lunch."

Kevin mimicked her action and checked his watch. "Oh yeah, I guess you're right."

Meg hadn't been this close to Kevin as an adult. When they were in middle school, he was a half foot shorter than her with braces and a stocky build. Now, he stood almost a foot taller than her and his stocky stature stretched to a muscled physique. He'd become a handsome man.

Despite his attractiveness, Meg remembered how mean Kevin was to her when they were in middle school and his constant taunts. "Spindly Legs Megs" and "Mega Monster" were what he called her. Oddly, this was how she'd become close with Ciara. Ciara, being the older twin of the two—by twelve minutes—knew how to put her little brother in check, which she did right in front of his friends on Meg's behalf. Ever since then, Kevin kept his distance to avoid his big sister's ire.

While they both went to the same high school, they didn't cross paths often. He played sports, she didn't, and the only thing they had in common was Ciara.

"I guess a coffee break makes sense." He hedged.

Meg smiled, aware of his attempt and certain she was no longer "spindly legs Megs"

"Sure. Coffee would be nice."

"Great! I have to drop this off in my office and then we'll have coffee. I'll be back in less than five minutes," he said then flashed five fingers.

"Okay. I'll wait here." Meg crossed her arms and watched

as Kevin hustled around the revolving doors, and, as promised, returned in less than five minutes.

"That was impressive. A politician who keeps his promises."

He grabbed his chest dramatically "Ouch, that hurt, but I guess I had that coming."

"Why would you say that?"

"You mean to tell me you don't remember how mean I was to you in middle school?"

"Oh, when you called me Mega Monster, and all those other awful names."

Kevin looked sheepish and stuffed his hands into the pocket of his chinos. His face turned an adorable light pink.

"Um… I guess you do remember."

"I do, but we're not in middle school anymore. So where do you want to grab some coffee?"

"How about across the street at Dippin' Donuts?"

Meg smiled and pushed a curl behind her ear. Both she and Kevin walked to the corner and crossed over to the donut shop. It was a local favorite and brimming with customers getting their mid-morning caffeine fix.

Meg walked up to the counter and browsed the menu. Kevin waited behind her. She felt his presence and without looking at him knew he was aware of her too.

"Welcome to Dippin' Donuts what can I get you?" asked the young girl behind the counter.

Meg glanced up at the menu one more time. There were so many choices of lattes and coffee. She decided to keep it simple. "I'll have a black coffee with cream and two sugars."

The cheerful worker rung up her order. "Yes, ma'am anything else?" Meg pointed behind her toward Kevin.

"Hello, Mayor, what can I get for you?"

Kevin gave the woman an easy smile, greeted her by name, then ordered a coffee and an old-fashioned donut.

"The regular?" she asked, and Kevin nodded.

Kevin waited and gestured for Meg to go before him to pick up the orders waiting at the end of the counter. They found a small two-seater table near the window to sit down.

"So, Mayor Kevin, you know everyone in town?"

"No, just the important people who make this town the great place it is."

Meg tilted her head and swung her bob to the side, looking from her coffee to Kevin, who suddenly seemed to be without words.

"I heard you're running for mayor again?" Meg said, then took a sip from her cup.

Kevin seemed to relax with this topic. "I sure am. It's one of the best jobs I could have. I like everything about it: serving the people, making Bluewater a better community, and meeting folks."

"That's commendable. Who would have thought you'd go into politics... but then again, you were pretty popular in school."

He blushed again, making it the third time since they bumped into each other. Meg didn't intend to embarrass him and figured she'd keep the conversation about the present. "So, I overheard Ciara say you're working for the library. How's that going?"

"Actually, it's not going. I was furloughed, and that's why you see me here today. I went to see about working again... had a meeting with the director which I don't think went well."

Kevin stroked his bearded chin, then leaned back in his chair. "So, you're not working?"

"Nope, not as of right now." Meg crossed her legs, took a sip from her cup and said, "What's up with you and Ciara? She always seems so mad at you."

Kevin tore open a packet of sugar, sprinkled it in his

coffee and swirled the cup then looked up at Meg. "She thinks I don't care about the town and that I'm going to run it to the ground. You know, she was actually my advisor for a while, but we butted heads on my vision… my promise to the town, so I had to fire my own sister. You can guess how that went."

Meg nodded her head. "Now I get it."

"I hated to do it. She's so smart, but unbelievably stubborn. There was no way we could continue to work together to see my promise through."

"Promise?"

Kevin took a sip then put his cup down with a grin. "Yes, it's the platform I ran on that won the election. I promised to move Bluewater into a stronger economic position with updates to its infrastructure. It's a beautiful place, but you may not know how badly we need updates in all of the systems. We are sorely behind the times."

"Wow, I didn't know that."

"And that is where Ciara and I bumped heads. She thought change would destroy our way of life and refused to look to the future."

"I had no idea how far apart you two were in thinking."

"Well enough about my opinionated sister. Are you looking for a job?"

"Sure. Do you know of anything?"

Kevin leaned toward Meg, giving her a whiff of his spicy scented cologne. "I actually have a position opening up in the mayor's office… its contractual, so there are no benefits, but it pays very well. The job is heavily research oriented. Does that interest you?"

Meg's eyes lit up while a large grin spread across her face. "That sounds amazing. I mean, research is what I do at the library… Wow! I could kiss you, Kevin."

Kevin blushed again.

Meg covered her mouth. She could have kicked herself.

"I'm sorry to have said that. Thank you."

"No problem. So, if you give me your email address, I'll send you a job description and a link to the application." Kevin reached into his pocket and pulled out his phone. He looked at the screen; his eyes grew wide.

"Oh, I have a meeting in five minutes. I nearly forgot about it." He tapped his contacts icon and gave Megan his phone. "Put your email in here and I'll send the info to you no later than tomorrow."

Meg took the phone and typed in her information then returned it. "No assistant to take care of these details or manage your calendar?"

Kevin rose and winked. "That job is open too if you're interested." It was Meg's turn to blush.

"Oh, I'll stick to the research job."

"Great. I'll take the job off the board. Thanks for having coffee with me. Sorry to drink and leave, but we'll talk soon. I just called you, save my number.," he said and hurried out the door.

Meg smiled, lifted her cup in his direction, and watched him leave.

It was all too perfect, she thought, "Now all I have to do is tell Ciara that I'm working for her brother." Meg sighed.

* * *

Dim lights shone through the windows of The Blue Lobster. It wasn't quite lunchtime, but the cafe would be opening soon. Meg saw Ciara's car parked on the side of the building. She was always there early and stayed late.

The Blue Lobster was Ciara's life and Meg wondered if her friend ever considered another one. One with a partner or children even. Ciara had boyfriends in the past, but they certainly needed to be strong to tolerate or handle Ciara's fire. There was one guy in particular who everyone knew was the one including Ciara, but he died in a motorcycle accident.

Ciara seemed to close herself from other romantic possibilities after that and buried herself with work. She opened The Blue Lobster the following year.

Meg made her way around to the front of the cafe. She peered around the etched Blue Lobster marking on the glass door.

Ciara fussed around the dining room, directing a few of the workers while removing chairs from the tables. Meg tapped on the door, causing Ciara to look up. She grinned, then walked over to the door.

"Hey, Megs, what's up? Come in." Ciara held the door open so Meg could enter, then locked it.

"Good Morning. You look happy." Meg removed her purse and tucked it in a nearby chair.

"Yeah, It's been a good day." Ciara smiled.

It was nice to see her in a good mood and hoped it would help when she told her about Kevin.

"Sure. If you want, grab one of those cloths and wipe down the tables. We'll be opening soon."

"Okay. I can do that." Meg stepped over to the bar and helped herself to a white rag from a pile.

"What are you doing here so early?"

"Just thought I would stop by since I was out earlier this morning."

"Out?"

"Yeah, I actually had a meeting with the regional director about my job."

"Oh, how did it go?"

"Well, I'm not sure. I'd like to believe it went well, but we'll see. I'll give him a call tomorrow morning."

Ciara moved around the room, picking up salt and pepper shakers and swiping beneath them. Meg tried to keep up and mimic her pace.

"Guess who I ran into at the offices?"

Ciara looked up, but kept moving. "Who?"

"Brandon. He didn't see me though, and it was probably for the best. He seemed to be preoccupied with keeping up with some woman." Meg stopped wiping and faced Ciara, her arms folded across her chest.

"Ah, Megs, I wouldn't worry about it. He was likely sucking up. You know how he is. On second thought, maybe you don't." Ciara chuckled and Meg tossed her cloth in her direction.

"He's not perfect. Yes, I know that, but he's not the worst either." Meg walked back over to the bar for another cloth.

"Can you grab another one for me too? These tables are dirtier than usual." Meg pivoted back for another and walked it over to Ciara.

"Guess who else I saw?"

"Well, I don't know... Santa Claus?"

"No, but that would've been nice... Kevin."

Ciara paused and looked over her shoulder. "My brother?"

"Yes, Kevin, your twin brother."

"Humph..." Ciara went back to rubbing the table with a little more force than earlier.

"He's really a nice guy. I mean he was a real jerk when we were younger, but Kevin's changed a lot and he's kinda hot too."

"Well, Megs, he's still a jerk in my book and I have no comment on his appearance other than he could use a shave."

Meg joined Ciara on one of the larger tables. "Why are you so harsh about him? You two are siblings... twins, even. Don't twins have a special connection or something?"

"Well, maybe some twins, but when you have a traitor for a brother, then the connection thing gets broken. You know, I really prefer not to talk about my brother. He's not one of my favorite people for a number of reasons and it's tough enough living in the same town, never mind he's the mayor of it."

Meg glanced at Ciara's tight lips and kept quiet, while wiping the opposite end of the larger table. She wanted to tell her about the job offer and now had doubts about telling her and even taking it.

Would it be wrong to keep it a secret? Should she decline Kevin's job offer?

It was as if she was being uprooted again. Just like when she was a child moving from place to place. She hated moving and all the new beginnings that came with it. Beginning new schools, trying to meet new friends she'd likely not see again after the next move. Even though she was an adult and had more control than she did as a child, it still bothered her.

All she wanted was a stable job and to keep her home. Was that too much to ask?

Meg exhaled. "God, I hope this other job comes through."

"I'm sure it'll work out, Megs," Ciara reassured her.

"I hope you're right. I'm running out of options here and everything seems like a compromise."

"Life is all about compromise and good food, ha! This place looks great… time to unlock the doors. Megs, do you mind?"

"Sure." Meg tossed her cleaning cloth to Ciara and strode to the front door to unlock it. The sun shone brightly through the front windows and glass door. The light hit The Blue Lobster etching, casting a diffused glow into the dining space. Meg looked up and noticed the window was clear. "What happened to your sign?"

"I took it down. It wasn't helping the business so, I came up with another plan."

"Another plan for what?"

"It's not fully formed yet, but trust me, I haven't lost my mojo for the cause."

Meg laughed. "I don't doubt it."

"Is there anything I can help you with?"

"Yeah, don't vote for my brother at re-election time."

Meg pursed her lips. "Where did that come from?"

"Just sayin'."

"Okay, I hear you…"

Ciara leaned both hands on the table and shook her head. "I'm sorry, Meg. That was harsh, and I don't want to put you between our issues. Just forget I said that." Ciara looked at Meg and gave a half smile. "Okay?"

Meg smiled back. "All is forgiven." Meg walked over and hugged her friend.

The door opened and an older couple walked in. Ciara went immediately into hostess mode.

"A table for two? Would you like a seat by the window?"

Meg waved to Ciara. Another group of people walked into the cafe and Ciara got lost in the activity of her business. Meg grabbed her purse from the chair and slipped out the front door as another patron walked in. She made her way to her car and hopped in. Meg pulled out her phone and scrolled for Kevin's number.

She contemplated her job rejection. Ciara's friendship was too important and a job would come along while good friends don't. She clicked on his number. It went straight to voicemail.

"Hey, Kevin, um, thanks for the job offer, but I'm going to have to turn it down. Something else came up and I won't be able to work for you. Thanks again and coffee was great."

Meg dropped the phone in her lap, then leaned her head back against the headrest and huffed.

"Something's gotta give." Meg put the key in the ignition and backed the car out of the parking spot, then turned on Main Street to head home. Her phone buzzed with a call. Meg looked down on the arm rest and Brandon's name popped up on the screen.

Meg rolled her eyes. "What does he want?" She let it go to voicemail and continued her short ride home. Meg parked in her usual spot and saw Trixie waiting patiently outside the door.

"Oh Jeez! She must have slipped out this morning." Meg threw the car in park and jumped out, rushing to the front steps. "Trixie girl, what are you doing out here?" Meg bent down and rubbed her head. Trixie looked from Meg to the door.

"I know, but you shouldn't be out here in the first place." Meg dug in her bag and pulled out her key. Trixie scratched at the door, then lowered her tail and crouched.

"What's wrong, girl… something got you spooked?

Heavy steps approached from the rear. "Hey, Meg, I've been waiting for you."

Meg spun around. Her hand flew to her chest. "Sheesh, Brandon! You scared me and Trixie."

"Sorry about that. I don't think Trixie was scared. She doesn't seem to like me very much."

"Not true, Trixie likes everybody." Meg opened the door and watched Trixie hightail it inside."

"Did you get my call?"

Meg scratched the back of her neck. "I… uh… was driving when you called."

"Right… can we talk? I heard you were at the office today."

14

"Sure. Do you want to come in?"

"Yeah, that'd be nice."

Brandon trailed in behind Meg, then closed the door behind him.

"It's so different during the day. You have nice light."

Meg placed her bag on the couch and scanned for Trixie who was likely hiding in the guest bedroom. She didn't want a repeat of what happened at Brandon's last visit.

"I like it too. Do you want to sit down? " Meg gestured to the chair. She was curious about why he came to see her, but she had her suspicions. It certainly wasn't to talk about the lighting in her place. "Can I get you something to drink?"

Brandon stood in place near the door. "No thank you. I shouldn't be here long."

"Okay. What did you want to talk about?"

Brandon shifted then sat down in the chair closest to the door. This must important. Meg sat down on the sofa across from him.

"I heard you had a meeting with the director. He called me into his office after you left."

"Really?" Meg leaned toward Brando. "So, I made an impression. What did he say?'

"Yeah, I'd say you made an impression." Brandon smirked.

Meg shifted and leaned back in her seat. "Is that a good thing?"

"Let's just say he found you forward." Brandon bent his finger to make air quotes.

"Well, I wouldn't need to be if you'd only put in a good word for me."

"How do you know I didn't?"

"He told me." Meg said and raised an eyebrow. What could he say to that? There was no way to dispute what she heard directly from his boss.

"Wait, I, I uh planned on talking about it at our next meeting. You know, I just got called back in the office myself. These things take time."

Meg stood and crossed her arms. "Come on, Brandon, I'm not an idiot. I saw someone there from the branch and she was furloughed too, then told me you brought her in."

Brandon dropped his head and slowly shook it. "So, you think I have that kind of power to bring in teams of people."

Meg bit her lower lip. "Well, yes, don't you have some say about who's on your team."

"Meg, you're more naive than I thought. I can't tell the boss to put this person or that person on my team. Maybe I can make suggestions, but he makes the final call."

"Oh, I just thought you could choose your team..." Meg's voice trailed off.

"That's fine, I get it. It's hard waiting to hear about whether you have a job or not, but be patient."

"Wait, what do you mean whether I have a job or not? It's when I get to come back to work."

"Yes, you're right. That came out wrong."

Meg ran her hand over the chenille throw on her sofa,

trying to let the repetitive motion and soft texture calm her. She wasn't sure about so many things now.

"Well, anyway, I'll call tomorrow to see when I'll be able to come back. It'd be nice to work in the main offices too."

"You want to work where I work?"

"Sure. why not? It'd be nice to work together again. Don't worry, I won't get in your way. I saw you today working with the director and some other woman."

Brandon cleared his throat. "Another woman… what did you see?"

"Nothing really. You came out of the director's office with a woman wearing a sweater like the one you bought me. I bumped into her on the elevator going up. She seemed nice enough. Is she new?"

Brandon rubbed his palms against his pants, then shrugged. "I guess. We recently met. The director put her in my group."

"Oh, okay. I saw you two leaving the office together and it seemed like…"

"Like what?"

"Nothing. It looked a little flirty, but I shouldn't be assuming anything." This wasn't important and Meg didn't want to look desperate like she had in the elevator. What she wanted was Brandon to save her job.

"You're right. It was nothing and let's not talk about it anymore. I came over here to see you."

"Thanks, Brandon. It's sweet of you to check on me. I've been okay, you know, spending time with my mom and friends."

"How's your mother doing?"

"She's great. She loves Allan and he's still calling orders." They both laughed.

"I remember you telling me about him. I'm glad you're spending time with your mom."

"We'll have to have lunch together, the three of us.

"Sure. we'll plan something." Brandon checked his watch, then stood. "I have an appointment to keep, but wanted to see you first. You look well, and hopefully, you'll get back to work soon."

Meg stood and led Brandon to the door. "I'm betting on it." She stopped and faced him. "And you'll do what you can to save it?"

"Of course." He said with a subtle flinch.

He walked out and Meg leaned on the doorjamb. "So, after your appointment, why don't you come by and we'll grab a bite to eat."

"Sure. If the appointment doesn't run too long, I'll call you."

Meg nodded and watched Brandon get into his truck. She closed the door and leaned against it. Trixie bolted down the stairs and made a hard turn into the kitchen.

"Trixie!" Meg called out. "What are you doing, girl? You don't have to hide, our company is gone."

Meg stepped into the kitchen. Trixie paced around her empty water and food bowl, letting Meg know she was hungry.

Meg took out a bag of dried cat food from the cabinet and poured some into her bowl. Trixie sniffed the semi-soft morsels then glanced at her water dish.

"Meow!"

"Sorry, it's all we can afford until I start work." Meg patted Trixie's head and caught a burr on her finger. She removed a second one from beneath her.

"Also, no more sneaking out. If I were working, you might not have gotten in the house until after dark. And you don't want to mess around with those coyotes."

Meg stood to check her closet for something to wear. If

Brandon's appointment ran short, she hoped they could have dinner tonight.

On her way to her bedroom, Meg hung her purse on the hook near the door. The blue folder poked from the top. It held her resume and reminded her about calling Mr. Harris tomorrow. She put the folder in drawer and sighed.

Would she get her job back?

15

The lights filtered through the blinds, waking Meg. She turned over and checked the clock. It was time to get up, even though she had no place to go... truly. She imagined that Brandon was in the office talking to Mr. Harris about her job.

Meg started a mental list of what she needed to do before going back to work. He was sweet enough to stop by and check on her yesterday. Even though he called to say he wasn't able to come back for dinner.

Meg pulled the blankets back, sat up, and stretched. Her stomach rumbled with hunger because of her early dinner. There wasn't a lot to choose from in the kitchen. She was too afraid to spend money.

She swung her legs onto the floor, walked to the window, and opened the blinds. Her bedroom faced the rear of the townhouse community which backed to a natural preserve. During some evenings, she'd hear the howl of native coyote packs and even saw a few in the past when coming in from late parties.

The packs seemed especially active last night. She fell

asleep past midnight waiting for the high-pitched barking and yips to stop. The creepy soul-haunting cries caused Meg to toss and turn. Their nocturnal songs were enough to spark nightmares.

Meg looked around. Most mornings she woke to Trixie's soft body slumped on her face. It wasn't her favorite way to be woken up, but she didn't have a choice in the matter. Meg looked around the room, but didn't see Trixie.

She was still bothered by the coyote's activity last night and rolled out of bed to look for Trixie girl. Meg checked the living room to see if she was sunbathing in the front window. Nope, not there either. She peeked in the kitchen and the other bedroom, but couldn't find her fur baby.

Meg's heart began to beat a little faster recalling how Trixie escaped the house yesterday and spent the afternoon frolicking outside while she was at her appointment. Had she gotten outside again last night without her knowing? Meg knew what happened to pets left outside accidentally at night.

"Trixie! Trixie girl," she called out, pulling back the curtains. Meg felt a tickle on her and looked down to see Trixie curling around her calf. She picked her up and scolded, "Don't scare me like that. I thought you pulled one of your escape tricks on me again."

Trixie batted at Meg's face with a furry paw. Meg smiled and placed her back on the floor.

Meg walked to the kitchen. "Let's see what's to eat this morning." Trixie trotted behind her.

Meg inspected her food bowl. "There's still food in your bowl. Waste not, want not. Sorry, girl. We can't afford to waste good food."

"Meow."

"There are little cats out there starving. You have a practically full bowl of food and are complaining."

Meg opened the fridge and pulled out a carton of eggs, milk set to expire today, and bread from the cupboard. "Looks like French toast this morning."

Meg mixed the eggs and milk together in a bowl and sprinkled in a little cinnamon. She pushed past spices in a lower cabinet to find some vanilla and added that to the mix.

"See how creative we can be when necessary." Meg continued with her cooking lesson for Trixie by adding butter to a pan she warmed on the stove. Trixie jumped onto the counter to get a closer look.

"Down, girl. It's not safe for you to be up here." Meg scooted her to the end of the counter and Trixie jumped down.

The smell of browning bread and cinnamon filled the kitchen. Meg's stomach rumbled, but with the satisfaction of knowing she would eat soon.

"All we need is some good ole New England maple syrup." Meg opened the fridge again, pulling out a half glass container of grade B amber maple syrup. She warmed it in a bowl of hot water. As a child she always picked the grade B syrup over grade A. It tasted like caramel to her.

Meg flipped the pan toasted bread onto the plate, plopped a pat of butter on each piece, then drizzled the warm syrup onto the eggy slices. Meg's mouth watered as she carried the plate over to the table. Trixie sat at her feet and stared up at the plate. Meg glanced at the dry cat food sitting in the bowl. Her heart pinged with guilt.

"Okay, just one bite and that's it. This food isn't good for you." Meg tore off a small piece and lowered it to Trixie's mouth, who licked at it, but did not take it from her hand. In fact, she walked away to eat at the dry mix in the bowl she'd previously ignored.

"So, that's how you're going to be— no more table food for you," Meg said and tossed the bread into the trash. She washed her hands, then sat down to enjoy the rest of her breakfast.

Meg rinsed off her dish and stuck it in the dishwasher along with the other dishes and cups. She'd turn it on once it was full. No point in wasting water or detergent. Meg's frugalness had kicked into high gear over the last couple of weeks. A leftover from her younger days of uncertain times.

She never expected to return back to those days of budgeting with ninja like precision. It was a necessary evil, and she ached for the times when she didn't have to check her account before buying a latte.

Meg closed the dishwasher and glimpsed at the kitchen clock. It was still early. She'd wait another hour before calling the director, giving him time to come into the office and settle. Sure this would give her brownie points for being considerate of his time and well-being.

Meg turned on the news and sipped on a glass of milk while watching the latest local happenings. By the end of the hour she knew it was going to be a sunny day with temperatures hovering around eighty degrees and water temps in the low seventies.

The Patriots were in training camp, and, as she suspected, Cape Cod's coyote population was growing and causing concern throughout the towns. Meg stood to bring her glass back into the kitchen when the phone rang. It was the director.

Meg's heart fluttered. Why was he calling her first? Maybe Brandon spoke to him about staffing first thing this morning. She clicked the phone and in the cheeriest voice she could muster said, "Hello."

"Good morning, this is George Harris. Is this Meg? asked the director.

"Yes, this is she. How are you, Mr. Harris?"

Meg sat back down on the sofa and listened to what the

director had to say. She slowly slid the glass back on the side table; tears filled her eyes.

* * *

Meg clicked off the phone and leaned back. Tears spilled over and streaked her cheeks. Her heart quickened as she sorted through her thoughts and feelings. "How could they fire me? What did I do to deserve this?"

The director spoke with reserved kindness and used words like "capable employee," "limited funding," "beyond his control," and finally "I'm sorry to lay you off."

Despite his cushioned statements, Meg understood she was being let go, fired, and all of those other ways to terminate employment, but what she didn't get was *why?*

Meg believed she'd done all the right things and spoke to the right people, but this was the result. The sun dimmed behind a bank of clouds, casting gloom into her home. She walked over to the windows and turned the blinds fully open to bring as much sunlight as she could back into the room. It helped a little.

Meg paced in the living room, debating who to call. Did Brandon know anything about this? No, he would have told her yesterday. She was certain.

Maybe it had to do with the developer and his plans to change the town, or even the new girl. She probably took her position, and they didn't have another one for Meg. Her head swirled with varied accusations.

Meg put on a pair of sweats, a T-shirt, and her Toms. She grabbed her sweater from the closet near the door and closed it. Trixie stirred from her nap. She needed some fresh air and someone to talk to. She knew who could give her perspective from the absurd thoughts swimming in her head.

Meg hopped in her car and headed toward Main Street.

As she drove past the now partially demolished library, her hands gripped the steering wheel. Meg was less hurt now, but felt a swelling anger bubbling on the inside.

She passed The Blue Lobster, which was still closed, then made a left at the end of main to Route 10. The road lined the coast and was a calming drive. She opened her windows to let in the salty air.

The briny scent from the bay revived Meg. In another ten minutes she arrived at the quaint entrance of The Bluewater Inn; Meg knew that Sharon would be up with her guests. She parked and got out of the car. It was a cool morning made brisk by the wind off the ocean. Seagulls cried and swooped into the water for the morning catch at the beach adjacent to Sharon's Inn.

Meg climbed the broad steps leading to the weathered oak wooden door. She tapped on the oval center glass and waited. When no one answered, she found the small door bell and rang that. A woman's figure approached the door and opened it. The smell of freshly baked pastries filtered through the air. Meg involuntarily licked her lips and smiled.

"Good morning, Meg, come in. What are you doing out this way?"

It was a funny thing to say since they lived in the same town, but Sharon was right. Meg hardly came to the Inn since they often met in town and most of what she needed was on Main Street.

Despite it being out of the way, this was a beautiful and less populated part of Bluewater. It lent itself to privacy that wasn't possible at the beach on her end of town.

"I was just driving by and thought I'd pop in. It smells like I came at the right time."

Meg walked into the vast foyer. The Victorian home was large yet quaint. Sharon spent a lot of time and an obvious amount of money to update and decorate it to reflect the era it was built. Meg loved how the large windows allowed swaths of light to filter in, always making it cheery and welcoming during the day. In the evenings, the inside lighting, gave it a warm and cozy feel.

"Yes, I was just pulling blueberry muffins from the oven. That's probably what you're smelling."

"Yum, I knew I smelled blueberries. Did you buy them from the farmer's market?" Meg had seen them last weekend when she visited the local farmer's market in town and but by the time she got over to the stand they were all sold out.

"In fact, I did. Come in and have a taste. I made enough for an army."

"Lots of guests this week?"

"No, I have a couple and someone in town for business staying in the suite. I had the urge for something sweet and needed to use up the blueberries before they wrinkled," she said with a smile.

"Well, since you have so many, I'll help you eat them."

The two women walked to the kitchen and settled around a large island filled with ingredients used for muffin making. Meg perched on a stool while Sharon heated water in the tea kettle. A low whistle let them know the water was ready.

Sharon poured a cup of tea for each of them and set the sugar and milk in front of Meg. She added four warm muffins onto a blue and white plate with creamed butter on the side.

Meg picked up a muffin and pulled it apart. Steam coursed up and the deep blue spots inside of the muffin oozed a sweet syrup. Meg used the small knife and added a dab of butter in the muffins' split and closed it. She waited for the butter to melt before taking a bite.

With a nearly full mouth Meg said, "Sharon, this muffin is amazing." She swallowed to clear her muffled voice. " You really should have your own bakery... a muffin bakery. You'd do so well."

"Thank you. You know that was one of my dreams as well as running my own inn." She gestured to the space around them. "I figured I could have the best of both worlds with the inn."

"Well, if you ever change your mind and want to open a bakery, count me in as your partner."

"Really, you'd leave your good state job for the uncertainty of entrepreneurship?"

Meg put down her muffin and sighed.

"That's actually the reason I came out here. I was fired. Well, in my director's words, 'laid off.'"

Sharon rested her cup on the saucer and tilted her head, giving Meg a sympathetic look. She reached for her hand and gently squeezed it.

"I'm sorry, Meg. When did this happen?"

"I got a call from the director of our department today, and I was completely blindsided by it. I had a meeting with him yesterday and did my best to be professional and assertive. We talked, and I promised to call today to see when I could return to work... and that was it." Meg shrugged her shoulders. "I don't know what went wrong, but now I'm officially jobless."

Sharon tapped her lips with the edge of the spoon and stared off in thought. "You know, Ciara has some interesting ideas about all of the changes that have been going on in town. She has been working on putting together some sort of task force to address the issues behind redevelopment, and I bet losing your job would be the proof she could use."

"Do you think it'd make a difference to become a part of this task force?"

"Well, I'm not sure, but Ciara has learned that if it weren't for the redevelopment, we would still have the library and you would have a job, but I'm far from an activist. So, don't take my word."

"I don't know about that. You confronted Chase Stiles on the beach at the concert, remember that?"

"Oh yes, I remember and he made me so stinking angry!" Sharon slapped the counter top. The tea cup rocked and spilled a little but teetered back on the saucer. Meg chuckled at Sharon's display of anger. "Oops," Sharon said and grabbed a napkin to wipe the puddle of tea.

"Well, maybe you're not cut out to be an activist, but we can be concerned citizens and call the office of Chase Stiles to talk about his intentions. Maybe there's a way we can all win."

"I like that idea. Let's call Ciara."

Meg nodded, then spoke with hesitation. "Maybe we should try it ourselves and tell her later."

Sharon's eyebrows raised, "I see what you mean… we might want to save the fire for when we need it."

"Exactly."

Both women laughed.

"Well, should we try to call now? There's no better time than the present."

"Sure. We have to do it quickly. I have new guests checking in today and need to do a few more things to prepare for their arrival. I think they're newlyweds." Sharon smiled and winked.

"Okay. Do you remember the name of his company?"

"No, but I have his card. He gave it to me that day on the pier. I nearly ripped it up."

Sharon walked to her purse and pulled out a neat mini card holder. In seconds she held the card in her hand. "Here it is. Do you want to call, or should I?"

"No, you do it. I'm still rumpled over today's news and you're always more cheerful than me."

"Oh really?" Sharon grinned and wriggled her brows.

"Would you call already? Here, use my phone."

"You really are grumpy."

Meg held the card and read the numbers aloud.

Sharon pressed the numbers on her phone and waited.

"Hello, my name is Sharon Stewart, and I'd like to speak with Mr. Chase Stiles... No, not a client. I'm the owner of The Bluewater Inn."

Meg sat on the edge of her stool with her elbows on the counter and her head resting in her hands. She watched Sharon intently.

Sharon's raised her brows. "He's available two months from now!"

Meg shifted in her chair and nodded. She mouthed "take it."

"Okay, I'll take that appointment. Yes, this is my number. Thank you for your help."

Sharon hung up the phone and glared at Meg.

"What? We had no other options. At least we're in the book and can always call back to cancel."

"We'll probably have a better chance of bumping into him around town."

"That's true, but now he'll see your name in his books and who knows what will come of it."

"Now look who's becoming the optimist."

Meg put her finger to her lips. "Shhh, don't tell anyone." Sharon chuckled.

"Well, I have to get a few things done before the guests arrive this afternoon. How about we meet at The Blue Lobster for dinner tonight around sixish?"

"That sounds great." Meg looked back at the remaining muffins and at Sharon.

"Would you like them in a baggy to go?"

"You read my mind."

Sharon walked to the other side of the long island and opened one of the many drawers on the side. She returned with wax paper and a paper bag. She wrapped the muffins like a gift.

"Here you go."

Meg took the bag, picked up her purse and headed toward the door. Sharon followed behind. Meg opened the door, then turned to face her friend. "Thanks for listening and the muffins too. It was what I needed."

"That's what friends are for, right?" Sharon said. "I'll see you at The Blue Lobster." Sharon nodded and closed the door.

Meg skipped down the stairs in a better mood than when she arrived. She opened her purse to store the muffins. Something stiff clung to the bag.

Meg still held Chase Stile's business card. It had his company's address printed on it. His office wasn't a too far drive and waiting two months to see him was beyond ridiculous. She'd think about it on the way to the grocery store.

What would it hurt to just show up at his office door?

16

Meg shook her hand to relieve the pain. The finger was red with a small cut where the door slammed on it. It wasn't serious and only needed a little peroxide and maybe a Band-Aid.

Only weeks ago, small mishaps like these wouldn't give her a second thought about going to see her doctor. Now that she was unemployed, Meg had to be careful. Not that she was particularly clumsy or uncoordinated, but that she couldn't afford to be careless.

Meg put the grocery bag down on the counter and walked to the bathroom. She opened the medicine cabinet and removed what she needed to bandage the cut.

"There, all better."

Trixie sauntered into the bathroom and looked up at Meg curiously.

"Hey, Trixie girl. I bought some of your favorite meals. The shrimp flavored one you love so much."

Trixie meowed and followed Meg from the bathroom to the front door.

"Wait inside while I get the other bags."

Meg walked outside and headed toward the mailboxes. She pulled out a handful of mail and flipped through the pile.

"Bill, bill, bill, ugh!" She stopped at an envelope with the state of New Hampshire seal. "What's this?"

Meg stuffed the other mail in the back pocket of her jeans. She opened the white envelope and pulled out the letter inside.

Dear Ms. Hollis,

Thank you for your application. We have reviewed over 100 candidates for the position of **Technical Services Librarian** and are pleased to offer you the job. We hope you continue to be interested in the position and ask that you contact our recruiter for the next hiring steps.

Congratulations and we look forward to hearing from you.

Sincerely,

Rudolph Simmons
Assistant Director of Human Resources

A warmth radiated through Meg and everything felt bright. She danced a one step in place, then jogged toward the house, reached the door, then went back to her car for the last two bags of groceries.

Meg's heart strummed in her chest. She could hardly believe her luck and wanted to shout, but didn't want her neighbors to think something was wrong, when in fact, everything was right. Well, almost right.

She walked back into the house, tossed the bills on the

counter and began to put the groceries away. Meg recalled the time she filled out the application.

She applied on a whim several months ago before she settled on the house. She was open to relocating. Plus, things weren't going well between her and Lucille. But then she met Brandon and found the perfect townhouse.

That seemed so long ago. What was she going to do? The job was in New Hampshire. Almost a three-hour drive one way, barring traffic. Meg shook her head.

"I'll need to move if I take this job."

Meg's elation dimmed. She hadn't considered leaving Bluewater and moving to another town for work. This scenario was all too familiar.

Her mother would get a new gig in another town or sometimes state. Often with less than a week's warning they were pulled out of their current life and on the way to a new one.

Lucille always hyped it as a new adventure. But Meg wanted friends and one place to call home, not the next greatest quest. She had that now with Sharon, Ciara and her mom here in Bluewater.

Meg loved knowing her neighbors and hanging out at the grill with her friends. Everything she needed was local and familiar. Could she leave this all behind for a big city up north?

Meg folded the letter and stuck it in the drawer. Trixie pawed at her pant leg and she bent down to pick her up. "Let's crack open a can of that fancy shrimp for you."

Meg was comforted by Trixie's appetite. She took large bites of the moist meal and didn't stop until it was finished. It pained Meg when she couldn't afford the kind of food Trixie would it. She felt like a bad mom.

"You were hungry," she said, and tossed the can into the trash. Meg finished putting the groceries away and saw a post office notice on top of the bills she tossed on the counter. There was a package that couldn't be delivered to her mailbox waiting at the post office for her. Meg glanced at the time, then stuck the notice in her purse. She'd pick it up later this week.

Sharon would be at The Blue Lobster soon. Even though it was a casual dinner, Meg felt the need to freshen up. She walked back to her bedroom and shuffled through her walk-in closet. Meg didn't have many clothes, by design, but owned a few classic pieces that she loved.

She pulled out a cotton button-down that tapered at the waist. Even though Meg wasn't keen on exercise, she'd inherited her mom's lean dancer's body. For now, sporadic workouts and walks along the beach helped to keep her in shape.

Meg took a quick shower, and washed her hair with the new shampoo she'd splurged on before losing her job. It filled the bathroom with a yummy berry scent that made her feel happy. After her bathroom routine, Meg dressed and was out the door. The sun seemed to be setting earlier, a sign of the waning summer.

It was the shortest season in New England and she lamented its end. Meg got into her car. Hunger pangs growled low in her belly. She started the car and steered it out of her parking spot, through her community, onto the main road.

She would arrive at The Blue Lobster early, but that was okay. Ciara would be there. Although Meg was eager to share the news of the job offer, she wanted to wait until Sharon was there.

Their opinions mattered to Meg. Ciara and Sharon were more like sisters than friends. They laughed like sisters, loved each other like sisters and of course disagreed like sisters. What would they have to say about the Meg's current dilemma?

* * *

Meg pulled into the lot and parked next to Ciara's car. She hoped it would be an agreeable dinner conversation. Meg was surprised and happy to see Sharon's car on the far side of the lot. She made it there early.

Meg got out of the car and straightened her cotton shirt. She loved the way the shirt felt, and the color was perfect. The problem was the wrinkles.

Meg pressed down on the shirt one more time to smooth it. The wrinkles sprang back, but it wasn't as bad as it could have been. She picked up her purse and hung it over her shoulder, then closed the car door.

The August humidity clung like an old wool sweater. Meg fanned herself, knowing it wouldn't make much of a difference. She normally entered from the front of the restaurant like the other patrons, but not today. Meg walked into the air-conditioned Blue Lobster through the rear entrance.

She took an appreciative breath, then pointed her attention to their usual table. Sharon and Ciara were already there and chatting. When Ciara spotted her, she waved her over.

"Hey, Megs, what took you so long?" Ciara teased.

"I'm not late. Sharon said around six o'clock and it's five fifty-five. So, I'm actually early," Meg said with a smile.

"Well, according to your military stepdad, five minutes before is on time and arriving on time is late," Ciara poked.

Meg rolled her eyes. "Oh, please, don't bring him up, and he is Lucille's husband not my dad in any way," Meg corrected Ciara with a certain head nod.

"Okay, just joking."

"What's got you in a good mood.?" asked Meg.

"Well, Sharon just told me what you two did today, and I think it's fabulous how fearless you are. It gives me hope that all is not lost in this town. If you are willing to face Goliath, then anything is possible."

"Gee, thanks… I think," Sharon said and took a sip of her lemonade.

"That looks refreshing. I'd like to order one."

Ciara caught the attention of one of the servers and called him over to their table.

"Yes, boss," he said, and Meg looked up to see the young lanky waiter with purple spikey hair.

"Hey your back?" she said to him. "You changed the color of your hair. It was…"

"Yes, ma'am, it was red. Can I take your order?"

"I'll start with a glass of lemonade like she's having." Meg gestured toward Sharon.

The young waiter turned toward Ciara. "Anything for you, boss?"

"Sure. I'll have a refill." Ciara handed him her empty glass. He looked in Sharon's direction with a questioning nod.

"I'm fine for now," she responded.

"Great, two old fashioned lemonades coming right up," he said and moved on to the next table.

"When did he get back?"

"Today's his first day back. He left for some family emergency, but things seemed to have cleared up."

"You're so kind, Ciara. Behind that tough skin is an old softy," Sharon said.

Ciara put her finger to her lips. "Shhh, don't say that too loud. You'll ruin my reputation."

Meg winked at Sharon. "I think we'd need to say more than that to change your reputation around here." They all laughed.

"So, what's new, Megs?" Ciara sat down in her usual chair facing the kitchen door. She could see all the workings of the restaurant from her vantage point.

"Actually, a lot. I got a job offer today."

Ciara and Sharon both rose from their seats and reached over to hug Meg.

"That's awesome, Megs!" said Ciara

"I'm so happy for you! We knew you could do it!"

Meg smiled and took in all of the well-wishing.

"Back with the library?" Sharon asked.

"That would be great to get your old job back, but you'll obviously have to work at another branch," said Ciara

"Wait, wait. Yes, I'm back with a library system, just not this one."

Sharon leaned in toward Meg. "Oh, well, where is it?"

"Yeah, Megs, don't hold back."

Meg raised her hands to block the onslaught. "Okay, okay, give me a chance. It's in New Hampshire."

Sharon's eyes widened. Ciara laid a hand on her forehead before speaking. "Gee, Megs, that's kind of far. How are you going to manage that commute?"

"I agree with Ciara. New Hampshire is almost three hours away, on a good day."

"Exactly, but I need a job and nothing is working out around here so far. What do you two think?"

"Well, I'm not sure what to tell you. I think it's a decision you'll have to make for yourself. I mean, I'd love to tell you what to do. But at the end of the day you'll have to live with your decision."

Meg turned to Sharon. "Well, what do you think?"

"This is going to be hard to believe, but I actually agree with Ciara for the second time tonight."

"I swear there must be a full moon. Just when I needed opinions, neither of you had one."

"What about your townhouse?" asked Ciara.

A tall frosty glass of lemonade appeared before Meg.

Startled, she turned around to see purple spikes move around to Ciara's side with her drink.

"Boy, you're really quiet," said Meg to the young man with the now purple hair.

"Will that be all, ma'am? Would you like to see a menu?"

"I think I'm ready to order too. Any specials?" Sharon asked.

"We have deep sea lobsters on the menu; straight off the boat this morning. The chef is making an amazing brown butter risotto with lobster as tonight's special," said Ciara.

Meg's mouth watered. "I'll have one of those."

"I'll have shrimp scampi," Sharon ordered

"Sharon, why don't you try something different. There are so many options on the menu," Ciara said.

"I know, but it fits my points for the day."

Ciara threw up her hands. "Have it your way." She turned to spikes who was poised with the pen and pad ready for the next order. "'I'll have the same."

He jotted down the orders, tucked the pad into his apron, and picked up the ignored menus. He left as quietly as he came. All eyes turned to Meg.

"So, what do you want to do?" Asked Ciara.

"I'm not sure, but I'm leaning toward taking the job."

"What about the commute?" Sharon's face was thoughtful.

"There wouldn't be a commute."

Ciara raised her eyebrows. "What are you talking about, Megs?"

"I'm going to put the townhouse on the market. I can't drive six hours a day, that's insanity."

"Are you sure that's what you want to do?" Asked Sharon.

"No, I don't want to sell. It's the first time I've had a real home. Lucille certainly didn't give us any stability. But you have to do what you have to do, right?" Meg lifted her glass to salute her decision, then took a sip.

17

Sharon giggled all the way to the car and leaned heavily on Meg's shoulder. She was sufficiently drunk. Halfway through the meal Sharon ordered a glass of wine then another before it was obvious she'd hit her limit.

Meg held her up as best as she could. "Sharon, you're hurting my arm," Meg squeaked from between pressed lips.

"Are you two okay?" Ciara called from the door and walked toward the duo. Meg shifted Sharon from her side to Ciara, who held her until Meg opened the door.

"I really love you two, you're the best friends a girl could ever have. Ever!" Sharon ended the phrase by thrusting her hand in the air, nearly knocking Ciara in the head.

"Whoa there, Sharon. Let's get you in the car, then home."

They managed to get her into the passenger's side without any other near misses.

Meg put on her seat belt, then closed the door. She turned to Ciara, who was scratching her head.

"I thought she only drank two glasses of wine. What happened?"

"You know Sharon's not a drinker. She's always had a

one-glass limit and that's with food. She barely touched her meal tonight."

Ciara lifted Sharon's doggie bag then looked from the bag to poor inebriated Sharon. "That makes sense."

She gave the bag to Meg, who put it in the rear seat.

"Thanks for dinner and drinks. I better get Sharon home. She's going to need the rest of the night and likely most of the morning to recover."

"All right, you got it from here, Megs?"

"Yeah, all set." Meg shook her keys and walked to the driver's side, opened the door, and slipped behind the wheel. Ciara walked back to the restaurant and watched them pull out from the door. Meg turned left on Main and north onto Route 10, driving past the pier and Amphitheater.

Through her open window, she heard the rhythmic roll of waves pushing up on the shore. The bay water was always relatively calm and more so on the northern end, earning its name: Serenity Beach. Meg focused on the road; only having a single glass of Merlot, she was unaffected.

Unlike Sharon, who fell asleep and snored in competition with Meg's engine. The road was empty with the exception of a few headlights that drove by on the opposite side of the road. Parked cars dotted the beach's seawall with obvious couples or small groups of clamorous teens.

Meg loved her town, and the idea of leaving weighed on her. Had she been the same Meg a year ago, there would be no questions about leaving. But now, she finally felt anchored, with a home, a community she adored, and friends she'd only grown closer to.

Meg's eyes watered. A single tear sprung and rolled down her cheek. She swiped it away. Sharon's place appeared in the distance. The outside lights gave the Victorian home a warm glow.

Sharon employed a cook and housekeeper to help

manage her guests and the property. They often did more and Meg guessed lighting the house this evening was the "more." She drove into the cul-de-sac of similar homes and looped around to The Bluewater Inn's front door. Meg looked over to see Sharon blinking her eyes several times. She took a breath while looking around in surprise.

"How did we get here?" She mumbled

Meg smiled. "I drove us here. You slept the entire way and even snored."

Sharon covered her mouth. "Oh, I'm so sorry. That was rude of me."

Meg waved her hand. "Don't worry about it, Sharon. I've seen and heard worse."

Sharon fumbled with her seatbelt. Seeing her frustration, Meg reached over and unbuckled it for her.

"Thanks, Meg. I think I may need your help up the stairs too."

"Sure." Meg got out the car and went to the passenger side. She opened Sharon's door and extended her hand. Sharon steadied herself then took Meg's hand. She stood quickly and seemed surprised to be standing. She held onto Meg and the two walked to the stairs. Sharon let go and held her balance.

"I think I can handle it from here," Sharon said and put one foot of the first of the wide planked stairs while holding onto the railing.

"Are you sure?"

Sharon looked to the top of the stair and saw the lights were on. She turned back to Meg. "Yes, I'm pretty sure, but you may not hear from me tomorrow." Sharon hugged her friend.

"Thanks for driving me home. You're the best."

"That's what friends do for each other."

Meg smiled and followed behind until Sharon reached

the porch. She wanted to be sure she made it safely in the house despite what Sharon said.

"Next time, only one glass of wine," said Meg.

Sharon turned around and gave Meg a thumbs-up, then turned the knob and entered the grand frosted glass door.

Meg got back in her car and pulled out her phone. She hadn't heard from her mother in almost a week. Although the dinner was a disaster, that typically didn't keep Lucille from checking in. Despite Meg's erratic relationship with her mother, Lucille reliably sought to stay in contact.

Meg sighed. Lucille didn't call, but she had missed another call. She listened to the message. It was from Chase Stiles' secretary. She asked if Sharon could meet with him tomorrow afternoon since he had a cancelation.

Why did he call Meg's phone and ask for Sharon? Meg remembered that Sharon made the appointment on Meg's phone and left it as the callback number. She knew Sharon wouldn't be up to the appointment tomorrow, and she didn't want to miss this opportunity to talk with the developer.

She'd tell Sharon about it after the meeting. Meg tucked the phone back in her purse and planned to call and confirm the appointment early tomorrow morning. Meg turned on the car and drove back down Route 10.

Fewer cars were parked along the seawall than just a bit ago on her ride to Sharon's and the rowdy teen scene dissipated. She turned on Main Street, passing the Dippin' Donuts where Meg could count on her pumpkin spice latte in the fall and a frothy hot chocolate in the winter.

Just beyond the donut shop stood several clothing boutiques that she and her mom would shop at on the Saturdays Meg didn't work. She drove past the rest of the familiar strip. Each part brought back memories or hopes of what she planned to do here in Bluewater. The Blue Lobster Grill was dark and Ciara's car was gone from her parking spot.

Meg was connected to this town. They had history and a future. Could she leave it that easily? It would be hard, but maybe, just maybe, tomorrow's meeting might change everything.

Everything meaning the future of the town. Was she doing the right thing going alone? Would she ruin any chance of turning the development around? It was a warm night, but she was struck by a wave wave of cold.

Now Meg wasn't sure about meeting with Chase Stiles. She grabbed her purse from the back seat to hunt for his business card.

18

Meg took several deep breaths before approaching the glass and steel structure. She remained surprised at how quickly things were going and hoped she did the right thing meeting Chase without Sharon. She had called first thing this morning to confirm the appointment. His secretary said, "Mr. Stiles is expecting you." As if she didn't have a choice and he was blessing her with his time. What an ego.

Maybe she shouldn't have come. Flashes of the horrible meeting with Mr. Harris popped in her memory. There was still time for her to turn around. Meg sighed, grabbed the door handle, then released it. She took a deep breath and reached for it again, this time yanking it open and walking through before she changed her mind.

It was a vast space where windows replaced walls. Despite the light, the lobby felt cold. Stainless steel and nickel fixtures glinted under the artificial light. Spare pieces of contemporary furniture seemed baseless and floated in the middle of the space like a science fiction movie.

She hoped the designer of this building was not the same

one assigned to rebuild the library. While it was bright and clean, Meg's skin prickled at the feel of the space.

A bank of elevators sat at the far end of the lobby. Meg checked the time. She was ten minutes early. Meg pressed the up arrow and waited for the doors to open.

She didn't have to wait long. Meg stepped into the elevator, the doors abruptly closed behind her as if to seal her decision to move forward. She pushed the button for the tenth floor.

The doors opened to a space with an equally modern aesthetic as the lobby level. She walked off the elevator and scanned a digital directory of offices on the tenth floor. The screen flipped between images of businesses.

Meg knew Chase Stiles' suite number, but waited for the digital board to confirm it. She crossed her arms and waited and waited some more. She was so close, but could easily leave. No one knew she was there and doubted Chase Stiles would care whether she came or not.

The screen rotated back to a 3D logo of the company. "There it is," she mumbled, then followed the arrows leading to the left and down a long carpeted hall to suite 1089. Meg stood on the other side of the oversized door with her hands perched over the extra long vertical steel handles.

Did everything have to be so intimidating? Meg wrapped her hands around each bar and pulled. She pulled several times to the unyielding glass before noticing a small round silver doorbell to the left of the door. She rang it and the large doors cruised open.

Meg entered the office and approached a sleek and long receptionist desk occupied by a young man.

"Hi, I'm here to see Mr. Stiles." He checked a small screen, then faced Meg.

"Megan Hollis?" he asked.

Meg nodded her head. "Yes, that's me."

"He'll be with you in a moment," he said, then gestured to an area with an arrangement of low-profile sofas situated in front of a large screen displaying fantastic structures and virtual portfolios of the designers.

"Thank you." Meg sat down on the farthest sofa from the desk. A pile of architecture magazines piled on the table in front of her caught her attention. She picked one up and thumbed through it.

While mindlessly looking at the photos of some movie star's home renovation a buzz sound caused her to look up.

"Mr. Stiles will see you now." The young man gestured toward the door at the other end of the desk, then walked around with a lunch tote in his hand. He strolled past Meg and pressed the button on the side of the office door, then left.

Meg placed the magazine back in the pile and stood. She blew out a short breath and wiped the sweat from her brow. Meg was ready. She made her way past the empty desk, through the door into Chase Stiles' office.

* * *

THE SPACE WAS MAGNIFICENT. Just like the glass walls of the lobby, two of the three in the corner office framed the tenth floor view. Meg could see the marina from where she stood. Chase leaned on his standing desk as if posing for a style magazine. The man matched his surroundings. She wondered if he got out of bed each morning thinking how to complement his Barcelona Chair.

The standing desk was one of three in the room, including a drafting table and a small square metal one. He saw Meg looking at the shorter desk.

"It came with the space before I ordered new furniture and I decided to keep it. I eat my lunch there," he said with smugness. "Have a seat. Can I get you something? Water, coffee, tea?"

Meg walked farther into the room and took a seat beside Chase's lunch desk. It felt the most familiar to her. He sat down across from her.

"No, thank you. I'm not thirsty."

"Okay, I hope you don't mind if I have something to drink. Thirty-two ounces of water is my daily goal," he said, whipping out a water bottle from a hidden fridge under the desk then pouring a glass.

"No, that's fine."

Meg watched Chase take sips of his water while scrambling her brain to remember why she had come, alone, without Sharon. She hoped to not blow this one too.

"So, tell me, why did you want to see me? And what happened to your friend? She was the one to call right?"

Meg nodded. "Yes, yes she was, but we both called. She couldn't make it today, so I'm here for the two of us."

Chase steepled his fingers, then tapped them on his chin. "So, I'll cut to the *chase*." He paused and looked at Meg. She understood his attempt at humor, but wasn't charmed. He leaned back in his chair and continued. "Okay, I'm assuming you're here to talk about the plans for development of your town, and if so, I'm impressed with your loyalty."

"Actually, I am here to talk to you about what your plans are doing to the town. Buildings and places that are important to the residents are being replaced, current businesses are being impacted, and people are losing jobs."

He leaned toward Meg, putting one hand on the chair's armrest. "Did you lose your job, Ms. Hollis?"

"Well, um… yes, I did," she stuttered. "But that's not the point of my visit. I'm here to talk about Bluewater."

"What if I could offer you a job right here in my company so that you wouldn't have to take that job in New Hampshire? I'd let you work from home." Meg's brows knit together in confusion. How did he know?

Meg crossed her arms over her chest. "Again, I'm not here to talk about me. Sharon and I are concerned about our town and thought you should know how it's affecting the people. And how did you know about my job offer in New Hampshire?

"Oh, I know all about the people of the little town of Bluewater. I know about the little group of activists led by the owner of The Blue Lobster and her plans to form some sort of task force and seek injunctions yadda, yadda, yadda, but she's barking up the wrong tree. I'm just the developer, but it's a big project and I don't like it when the average man, or in this case woman, messes with my money," he said tapping a pen on the desk.

Meg felt like she was in over her head. How did he know this information? Meg didn't know about the task force and thought he might be blowing smoke.

"Look, Mr. Stiles, if you're not going to…"

An abrupt knock on the door caused Meg to pause and turn around. "Hey, I brought you that information you were looking for." Chase's eyes grew wide and he cleared his throat.

Meg turned to see the purple spiky hair waiter step into the room. Their eyes met with immediate recognition.

He backed out of the room. "Oh, I'm sorry… didn't know you were in a meeting." The door firmly closed behind him.

"So, as you were saying, Ms. Hollis. You have my full attention."

"I was saying that this meeting is over and I now know you can't be trusted and the town of Bluewater isn't for sale."

Chase shook his head. "Are you sure you speak for everybody?"

Meg stood up as Chase followed. She kept her hands

clasped in front of her. "Thank you for your time, Mr. Stiles. I'll see my way out."

He extended his hand toward her. "It was nice meeting you again." Meg kept her hands together refusing to shake his hand. He held it out for a few seconds more before dropping it by his side.

"I'm sure it was," she said, then turned and left the office. She needed to talk with Ciara immediately.

Did she know there was spy working at the Blue Lobster Grill?

MEG PHONED Ciara several times on the drive back to town. Each time it went to voicemail. She wanted Ciara to be aware of the spy in her midst, but Ciara wouldn't pick up. It was peak season and the restaurant was likely hopping with tourists.

Hopefully, Ciara wasn't having sensitive conversations around any other sneaky waiters spying for Chase Stiles. Meg should have trusted her gut. She knew there was something odd about him beside his hairdo, but couldn't put her finger on it.

The traffic backed up for what looked to be about a mile as soon as she made it to the Sagamore Bridge. Meg kicked herself for not timing her return home. Better yet, she should have requested a phone meeting, but that would not have been as effective and luckily she didn't. Discovering the mole was worth the hours she'd be spending in traffic on the way home.

Meg searched for a music station to help pass the time. She found one playing soft rock, but after one song a slew of ads followed. Meg switched to the news to hear traffic alerts, and the reports weren't good."

"Ugh, another reason to not commute," she mumbled to herself.

Meg turned off the radio and rolled down the windows. A bicyclist raced by on the pedestrian path of the bridge. She'd never do that and admired people with such audacity. The path did not have a barrier to separate it from the traffic. In her mind, she might as well jump from the bridge.

Meg changed her focus to the canal below. While inching across, she caught glimpses of the blue water and houses perched on the water's edge. Meg exhaled when her phone rang. It was Ciara. She switched the call to Bluetooth.

"Hey Ciara."

"Everything all right? You called a few times."

"I'm fine, but you'll never guess where I'm coming from and who I saw."

"I probably won't and don't have much time, so go ahead and tell me," she said brusquely.

Meg sensed Ciara was in a mood and thought she should wait until they were in person, but knowing Ciara there was no waiting to share news.

"Okay, I'm coming back from a meeting with Chase Stiles—"

"The developer? Why are you meeting with that scoundrel?" She interrupted Meg before she had a chance to finish telling her what happened.

"Yes, that scoundrel, and I'm telling you now. We had a meeting that Sharon and I set up."

"Is Sharon with you too? I should've been there."

"You know, it might be better if we talk about this when I get back to town."

"No, go ahead and finish. I'm listening."

Meg took another breath.

"Sharon couldn't make it. So I met with him by myself

and it seemed like a good idea at the time, but he is really a snake."

"What happened?"

"First, he seemed to know about my new job offer and offered me a job. Next, he talked about some sort of task force you were supposedly leading."

"Really? How did he know all of this?"

"Precisely. But wait, this gets better. As we're talking, the waiter from your restaurant walks in then quickly leaves."

"Are you saying the waiter is spying on me for Chase Stiles?"

"Yes!"

"Meg, that's a bit much. I mean, why would a big developer want to know about anything going on in a local restaurant?"

"He wants to keep us from stopping his plans."

"Well, he can't stop us and that poor kid is having family problems. I met his folks. He's not a spy. Maybe he's getting his info from Kevin. You know my brother is pro-development and likely giving him all sorts of information."

Meg quieted, and the traffic began moving. She didn't want to launch Ciara into a conversation about her brother; she wanted to keep the door on that topic closed.

"The traffic is moving now, so I'll need to pay attention to the road. Can we talk once I get into town?"

"Sure. But it'll have to wait until later. It's busy here and I've got to work on the books tonight, so tomorrow might be better."

"You don't believe me, do you?"

"Megs, I believe you, but the source may be different and honestly you need to stop being so gracious to my brother."

Meg shook her head. "This isn't about Kevin and you're not taking any of this seriously."

She waited for Ciara's response. "Megs, sorry to cut you

off, but it's picking up here and I have to go. Talk to you later."

Ciara hung up the line and Meg's jaw tensed. Chase had played a cool hand and belittled her attempts to save Bluewater from his development plans. She uncovered a spy in their midst, but her best friend blew it off. Nothing had gone as planned.

Taking the job offer and moving to New Hampshire might not be a bad idea.

19

Meg jerked the car to a stop. She didn't see the red sign at the intersection. Her mind shifted from Ciara's callous response to Kevin. Could he really be the source? It was a possibility, but Meg knew what she saw.

She was frustrated. Despite all of her efforts to do the right thing, she remained unemployed. Meg received three job offers over the past week and decided she'd accept one of them regardless of the repercussions. Her bills were coming due. The mortgage was past due, and if she sold the house it needed to be current.

Meg turned into the post office parking lot. It was closing soon, and she hustled to get inside. A woman dressed in light blue button down shirt and uniform pants stood at the door and waved for her to enter. She locked the door as soon as Meg got in and only allowed others to exit.

Meg stood in the short line and pulled out the certified mail notification along with her ID card. The postal clerk wearily called her over.

"How can I help you?" he asked.

Meg handed him the slip of paper and her license. "I have a package to pick up."

The clerk studied the notification, then left his post and returned with a large manila envelope." Please sign here, ma'am," he said pointing to the bottom of the slip then handed Meg the envelope.

She tucked it under her arm, then headed to the exit. The on guard postal worker unlocked the door and pushed it open for Meg to leave.

"Thank you," said Meg

"Have a good evening," she said before locking the door again.

The bulky package pushed against Meg's arm while she walked to the car. A cloud cover sprinkled drops of rain that soon turned heavy. Meg jogged to her car and got inside. She dropped the package on the passenger's seat, then started the car.

Several turns later, Meg was home. She gathered her things and let herself into the house.

Aa soon as she opened the door, a calico ball charged at her feet. She crouched and rubbed Trixie's back. "Hey, Trixie girl. I missed you."

Trixie purred.

A cat toy squeaked under Meg's foot. "You've been busy today."

Tired from the day's events, Meg fell onto the sofa. She wanted to eat dinner and fall asleep, then start again tomorrow, but she was curious about the package. Meg could see it from where she lay and tried to will it into her arms, but the package didn't budge. Unfortunately, she'd have to move. So much for those YouTube mind tricks tutorials.

Meg grabbed the package and plopped back down on the sofa. She flipped it over. It was from the mortgage company. Meg's heart dropped. She tore the envelope open and pulled out a letter. Meg scanned the first paragraph. Her hand flew to her mouth.

"Pre-foreclosure proceedings! They're going to take my house!"

Tears rolled down her cheeks. The mortgage was a month behind, but she didn't expect a foreclosure. What did this mean?

Meg read the rest of the letter. She had a chance to catch up on her payment before any other actions would be taken. Meg read the letter again and circled the number at the bottom of the page. She'd be calling tomorrow.

She grabbed the phone to call someone, then stopped. How could things have gone this far? She shook her head and released a deep moan. Meg couldn't let anyone know. She was supposed to be responsible.

The phone vibrated under her hand. She flipped it over. It was Brandon. She answered and put it on speaker.

"Hey, Brandon."

"Hi, Meg, how are you?"

"I'm okay. Just got in the house."

"I was thinking about you and thought I'd give you a call."

"Really? Are you bored or something?"

Brandon laughed. "Well, now that you mention it, I guess I am."

Meg frowned. "So, you only call when you have nothing else to do."

"No, it's not like that. Anyway, did you hear back from the director about the job?"

Meg's face warmed, and a flush crept across her cheeks.

"Oh, right… I guess you don't know." Meg shifted her legs. "I was fired."

"What? He fired you?"

"Well, technically it was a layoff, but it's the same thing. I don't have a job."

"Wow, Meg, I'm really sorry to hear that. It seems like it's happening a lot. My sister's roommate lost his job too."

Meg perked up. A roommate. Why didn't she think about that before? Meg had another room, and she was sure plenty of people would love to live near the beach. Meg added this task as a mental note to start her search tomorrow."

"Really? I didn't know she had a roommate. I hope things work out for him."

"I guess so."

"Having a roommate is a pretty smart idea to help with costs. What do you think?"

Brandon paused before speaking. "I think that works for her."

"I think it would work here too and it would be nice to have someone around." Megan gestured around her place.

"I can see how that would work for you."

"And not for you?" Meg said.

"Look, Megan, I can see where you're heading with this and I don't think it would be a good idea for us to move in together."

Megan's phone slipped out of her hand and bounced off the couch onto the floor as she covered her mouth from the rising chuckles. She picked the phone up.

"Hello, Meg… are you okay?" he said

"Yes, sorry. The phone fell from my hand."

"I hope you didn't take what I said too hard. You're a nice girl, but moving in isn't something I'm ready to do."

Meg bit her lip to keep the words she wanted to say from coming through. It was clear that Brandon did not attempt to help get her job back and suspected he played a role in her losing it. And now, in her moment of need, he wasn't willing to help. Meg knew it was time to change.

"I hear you, Brandon, but that wasn't my intention. In fact, things in my life are happening that need my attention and it wouldn't be fair to you for us to continue to see each other."

"Oh, really. Sure... I was actually going to suggest the same thing."

Meg smiled and shook her head. She was glad Brandon was on the phone and not standing in front of her.

"So, friends?"

"Yes, friends. And if you need anything, don't hesitate to call me," Brandon said.

"Certainly. You will be the first person I call."

"Bye now."

"Bye, Brandon." Meg clicked off the phone and tossed it to the side.

It was clear that Brandon wasn't on her side. Everything was a mess. What was she going to do now?

* * *

"Hey, Meg, I got your message and hope you change your mind. There's no pressure and I'll keep the offer open. If you decide otherwise, let me know by the end of the week. I would... um, we would love to have you on our team."

Kevin's voice was honest and authentic. He seemed remorseful about the way he treated her in middle school, and he called to offer the job again. Kevin was becoming hard to resist.

Meg paced the kitchen, listening to his voice message a second time. She thought about Ciara and what her reaction would be if she took the job. It had been clear for her the other day while she helped her clean the tables at The Blue Lobster, but she couldn't ignore the turn of events. Meg needed a job.

She needed another opinion. Someone to help navigate this conundrum. Sharon was likely still nursing her hangover, but it had been almost twenty-four hours since Meg brought her home. It was likely safe to call to check in at least. Meg scrolled down then tapped Sharon's number.

"Hey, Sharon, I'm just calling to check in. I hope you're feeling better. Call me when you can."

Meg clicked off the call when Sharon's name popped on her screen.

"I just left you a message."

"Sorry, I was talking to one of my guests and couldn't get to the phone in time."

"Always on the job."

"Yes, when you run your own business, that's what happens. So, what's up? By the way, thanks for bringing me home last night. It's been a while since I enjoyed wine and cocktails. I won't be doing that again too soon."

"I must have missed your cocktails. That makes sense though, I thought the wine alone did you in."

"No, no, it was the cocktails. Thanks for checking on me, but I'm fine."

"That's what friends do." Meg warmed on the inside, recognizing how much her friends meant to her. "Do you have a couple of minutes?"

"Of course. what's up?" Sharon asked.

"Well, I have a dilemma and you are always so great about seeing both sides of the issue."

"I'm not so sure about that, but go ahead, shoot."

"Okay. You know that I lost my job at the library."

"Yes, I still can't believe it happened."

"Right, and I got the offer in New Hampshire and thought that was my only option, but honestly, Sharon, Bluewater is my home and I don't want to leave."

Sharon sighed. "And I don't want you to go either. What can I do, Meg?"

"I need your honest opinion. Today, I received more bad news in the mail. My house is in pre-foreclosure."

A loud gasp echoed over the phone. "Oh, Meg, why didn't you tell me earlier? I can help you."

"Thank you, Sharon. I knew you'd offer, but I wanted to take care of this on my own. After all, I got into this mess by myself."

"What are you going to do?"

"Well, I may be able to stay in Bluewater, but it might cost me something that's important?"

"What?"

"A friendship."

"What do you mean? Everybody wants what's best for you, Meg."

"I hope so, because there was another job offer, right here in Bluewater."

"That's wonderful, Meg. Why didn't you tell us?"

"Kevin offered me a job." Meg switched the phone from one hand to the other, waiting for Sharon's response.

"Kevin? Mayor Kevin? Ciara's brother Kevin?"

"Yes, all of those Kevins."

Meg leaned against her granite counter. She expected Sharon's reaction, but hoped she'd see a way around the problem.

"I see what you mean about the cost of taking that job. Don't get me wrong, I don't have a problem with it, but Ciara, she might not take it so well."

"That's what I thought. So, what do you think I should do?"

"Meg, you have to do what's best for you and let Ciara sort out her own feelings. She may be angry at first, but I bet she'll come around."

"So, you think I should take the job?"

"Absolutely!"

Trixie sauntered into the kitchen and nuzzled at Meg's leg. Meg picked her up.

"Do you hear that, Trixie girl, we're staying here." Trixie squirmed out of Meg's arms, then jumped to the floor.

"Oh gosh, I forgot about Trixie. If I weren't so allergic to cats, I'd visit more often. Thank goodness for Zyrtec." Sharon laughed.

"It's fine. I understand and Trixie isn't offended, are you, girl?" Meg bent down and stroked Trixie's fur.

"Let's hope Ciara isn't offended when I tell her my choice." Said Meg.

20

Ciara flicked off the open sign. She arranged the chairs to face the table of appetizers, where she'd face the crowd. She closed The Blue Lobster early to prepare for the big meeting. Ciara planned all week for tonight and hoped for a good turnout. The meeting seemed like a natural progression to what the local patrons of Bluewater and Ciara debated.

It was nearly 8:00 p.m. Ciara closed the kitchen and paid the kitchen staff for the full night. She was thankful for her employees. They worked hard and were like a family. Ciara came from a family with an incredible work ethic and was competitive. She spent her formative years trying to prove her worth to a dad who pushed his sons to compete and but had fewer expectations for his only daughter. Ciara learned to play just as hard as her brothers. She became a high school all-star softball player and the student body president. Kevin was the vice president, but it was his opinion and take on things that seemed to capture his dad's attention.

In her final year of high school, Kevin decided he wanted to be the president, and the two ran against each other. It was a heated race and in the end Ciara got the victory. It was her win that strained the relationship with her father, whose words afterward were, "Why didn't you just let him win." She learned a few things about herself and it paved the way for her to start her own business.

Ciara looked around the room. The chairs were set up and ready for the invited guests. She put out an invite on the town's list serve to talk about the changes going on in Bluewater. Ciara wasn't sure what the turn out would be since she didn't ask anyone to rsvp, but based on what her customers said, it would be a decent turnout.

Ciara had the kitchen set a table of snacks for the expected crowd. She added a few more plates to the table, then checked the time. As if on cue, the door opened and a group of familiar faces trailed in.

"Hey, Ciara, said Mrs. Miller."

"Hiya, Ciara, where should we sit?" asked Ralph Buckley.

"Good evening, Ciara," said another. More greetings were heard as more folks arrived at The Blue Lobster. By half past the hour, the place was nearly full. She was amazed and humbled at the turnout. Neighbors and customers chatted over her mini sandwiches. Small clusters engaged in serious chats about the news of the day, and she overheard a group commenting on her food and sharing a recipe.

This was the town Ciara knew and grew up loving. She didn't want to see this community change, and by the turnout she guessed she wasn't alone.

Ciara cleared her throat, then raised her voice slightly above the crowd. "Thank you all for coming. If you'll have a seat, we can get started."

Everyone found a seat and settled in. Ciara stood at the head of the table of appetizers. She thought she'd be nervous, but it felt right.

"Again, thank you all for coming out. I know you could

have been doing any number of things at this time, but by being here it tells me a lot about how you feel about Bluewater."

"Save Bluewater!" exclaimed one of the seniors in the group who was as brazen as they come.

"Thank you, sir, and with the support of everyone here, that's what we intend to do."

A chorus of agreement went up along with a burst of claps.

Ciara waited until it died down before continuing.

"I put together a short agenda that is worthy of creating a task force. My intention is to identify all of the problems and issues development is bringing to our town and address them at every turn."

Another burst of claps erupted. Ciara paused, then passed around a list of items she intended to talk through. The room quieted as each person read through the list. Ciara watched their faces, then listened as the comments came.

"Good ideas," said Nancy.

"Can we do this?" asked Simon Fishler.

"Do we have the authority to make this happen?"

"I like your gumption, Ciara," said the brazen senior

Ciara stood straight and pushed her shoulders back. She smiled at the crowd before going on.

"I know it seems like a lot to accomplish, but if we come together in small groups within this larger with each taking on one of these tasks, then I'm certain we'll make things happen."

"Ciara, I like your ideas and think they'll make a difference, but this seems like more of a platform," said Nancy.

Ciara nodded her head. "We can use this as a draft and make changes. This is just a start."

Simon looked at the paper, then stood up beside Ciara to

scan the crowd. He turned to Ciara and said, "I have a better idea."

She studied Simon's earnest face. "And what's on your mind?"

"I know your intention was to start a task force and we are here to support that idea, but wouldn't it be easier to make these changes from the mayor's office?"

Ciara inhaled, then slowly released her breath. "I certainly can invite the mayor to the next meeting, if that's what you want."

She saw a few head nods before Simon shook his head and looked back at the crowd. "Actually, that wasn't what I was thinking. We all know that Mayor Kevin wants to see these changes. He's a nice guy and we all respect him, but your ideas are our ideas and…" He turned to the crowd almost as if to be looking for their blessing. "If the group agrees, we'd support you if you ran in the upcoming election for Mayor."

The room erupted in cheers and claps, then stood up as an endorsement. Ciara had no idea this was coming. Her cheeks flushed a deep warmth which told her she was the color of the strawberries sitting on the table beside her. Ciara's hand flew to her chest. Her heart thumped as she searched for a response.

"I am honored that you would propose such a thing, but to make a political run is a big deal. My hope this evening was to form a task force, and I know this list may seem tough to do, but I know we can do it together."

"Come on, Ciara! You're a natural, you can do it," yelled Joe from the donut shop.

Ciara smiled and shook her head. "I don't know. How about we talk about some of these issues before it gets too late."

Simon patted Ciara on the back, then sat down. Ciara looked over the supportive crowd then leaned with confidence on the table behind her. She gazed down at the agenda that had the makings of a political platform.

Hmm... Mayor, she thought.

21

Meg drummed her fingers, waiting for someone to pick up the line. She woke up this morning energized to work her plan and the day started well. Meg called Lucille, who seemed happy to hear from her. They spoke for a bit and then planned for Meg to head over there later.

Sharon's pep talk helped to make up her mind. Meg also guessed that was part of her wistful attitude. She put the phone on the table and took sips of her coffee.

"Good morning Baylor Bank, can I have your account number please."

Meg picked up the phone, took it off speaker and held it to her ear. Trixie tilted her head and looked at Meg curiously. Meg turned her back to the cat and rattled off a long series of numbers.

"Yes, that's me, Megan Hollis."

Meg shifted in her chair and reached for a pen until the representative finished updating Meg on her history with the bank. She was well aware of the missed payment and what her obligations were.

"Yes, I received the packet and that's why I'm calling. I'm recently unemployed and..." Meg nodded as the young woman explained her options that she was glad to hear.

"So, it's possible to delay a payment, but the remaining monthly payments will be slightly increased for several months," Meg repeated. She thought this was a fair solution, but needed to make sure she'd be working soon. She listened and jotted down some notes while the bank representative explained what Meg needed to do next.

"Thank you for your time and help." Meg finished the call and hung up. She stretched her arms and yawned. The day was still early, but yet felt like she'd run a mental marathon. She stood up and emptied her coffee cup in the sink.

"Okay, Trixie girl, I'm off to Lucille's."

Meg walked into the living room, grabbed her bag, and checked for her keys before heading out of the door. She was hopeful to have a good visit with her mom. Sergeant Allan was out of town, and Mom always seemed to be less anxious when he wasn't around.

As Meg got in the car and turned on the ignition, a red light blinked to remind her she was low on fuel. In the past, she'd drive around town without a second thought to these minor expenses. Now she considered all costs, and unfortunately most of those costs were now put on her credit card. Meg shook off the thoughts that followed and planned to stop at the gas station on the way back from Lucille's. She'd worry about the growing credit card balance later.

Meg pulled out onto the main road. She managed to drive down Main Street without dread as she passed the nearly demolished library.

"Such a shame."

Meg took a shortcut to her mom's which took her by Serenity Beach. It was another beautiful day, and she could see a line of cars parked along the seawall. Meg thought it would be a great day to have dinner at the clamshell. She'd call Sharon after visiting her mom.

Meg pulled in beside the tank. Allan must have flown out of town and left it behind. She often wondered what it looked like inside and if he outfitted it to look like an actual war vehicle. The tank was intimidating even though it was only a pimped out SUV.

Lucille stood at the front door and waved to Meg. She must have heard her car pull into the driveway. Meg waved back and got out of the car. Lucille smiled at her as Meg walked up.

She leaned in, and the two hugged. "Hello, sweetheart."

"Hi, Mom, how are you?"

"I'm good now that you're here. Let's go inside."

Meg followed Lucille through the handsomely designed foyer. Lucille's background as an artist influenced the space's design. Abstract sculptures dotted the room, revealing her passion for modern art. Lucille led her into the kitchen where Meg could smell coffee brewing and noticed a brand new sparkling espresso machine sitting on the counter.

"Wow, Mom, that's impressive. When did you get that beauty?"

"Allan bought it for us. After our trip to Italy, he's been on a mission to recreate those delicious cups of coffee we had over there. Do you like it?"

"Yes, it's very nice, but looks complicated. Do you know how to use it?"

"Well, for the most part. Do you want a cup?"

"Sure, I'll try one."

Lucille walked over to the machine and Meg followed. She placed an espresso cup under one of the spouts and fumbled over the levers. Meg looked over her shoulder.

"I think you press this button here and…" A burst of steam shot out of the spout. Lucille jumped back into Meg and they both nearly fell to the ground. The machine hissed angrily, and Lucille moved to shut down the angry machine. They leaned into each other laughing.

"Mom, that was awful. Are you okay?"

Lucille wiped her hands on a cloth sitting on the counter. "I think so, but I'll wait until Allan comes back before fiddling with that thing again." Lucille gestured toward the table.

"Have a seat while I get our lunch. We'll eat by the pool; the weather is gorgeous today."

"Can I help with anything?"

"Yes, you can carry out the drinks." She pointed to a tray holding glasses and a round pitcher of Meg's favorite iced tea.

"Got it." Meg slipped her hands through the tray's handles and walked through the patio doors and onto the tiled deck. It was a beautiful setting. Lucille planted annuals in the beds on the far side of the pool. They bloomed lively pink, purple, and yellow flowers which intentionally complemented the cushions of the patio furniture. The pool's surface shone like a smooth plate of glass waiting to be broken.

Meg and Lucille spent several lazy Saturdays by the pool's edge, in the water or in the attached hot tub. Meg could not have imagined this when she was younger. Lucille did not have means to provide this lifestyle for her two girls as a single mom. Megan thought the invites to spend time with her at the house might be Lucille's way of making up for that.

Megan placed the drinks on the table closest to the pool under a wide umbrella. Lucille walked up and added a plate of lobster rolls and an assortment of sliced raw vegetables.

"That looks yummy. Did you make the lobster salad yourself?"

Lucille grinned. "No, I bought it from the deli. But I did add them to the rolls," she said with a satisfied smile.

"Bravo, Mom. I'm sure it will be delicious."

Lucille picked up one of the rolls and took a bite. "Mmm, it is tasty. Try one. I don't think you'll have to worry about it hissing at you." She chuckled.

Megan was glad to be spending time with her mom and cherished seeing her happy. She picked up one of the rolls and bit into it. "Mmm, these are good and no hissing, but I'll have to come back once you learn how to tame that espresso machine." Meg pulled a chair away from the table and sat down. She placed the half-eaten lobster roll on a plate and added carrot sticks. Lucille sat down too and turned her chair to take advantage of the light breeze.

"So, did you hear back from your job? When will this furlough be over?"

Meg looked down and pushed the few carrots around on her plate. "Mom, I lost my job."

Lucille's mouth fell open and she reached for Meg's arm. "I'm so sorry, honey. When did you find out?"

Meg shrugged her shoulders "The other day. I got a phone call from my boss and he said I was laid off."

"I can't believe this. Is there anything I can do?"

"Well, a small loan would help until I get on my feet."

Lucille looked out of the pool. "Oh, honey, I don't know. After you refused to apologize Allan said you didn't deserve the money and if you apologized later, he'd doubt it'd be sincere and only out of desperation…" Lucille's voice trailed off.

Even when out of town, Allan still managed to irk her and control Lucille. "Well, I'm not desperate and I don't need Allan's money!" She huffed.

"Megan, I'm not trying to anger you, but if you weren't so stubborn you could've had the loan," Lucille said, throwing her hands up.

"It's fine, Mom. I'll make it work."

"Look, sweetheart, I have some money in my account that you can have and I'll work on getting you more. I just wish you weren't so difficult all the time. Is that what caused you to get laid off?"

A bark of laughter escaped Megan's mouth. "Are you serious? You are blaming me for getting furloughed then being laid off. You are unbelievable, Mom." Megan pushed herself up from the chair and narrowed her eyes at Lucille. "I wouldn't take your money even if I landed on skid row. Goodbye, Mom!" she said, then snatched the lone lobster roll off the plate before marching off to the kitchen through the house and out the front door to her car.

Megan smashed her finger against the car key button several times to open the door. It took a few tries before she heard the click. Meg rushed into the car, dropped the lobster roll in the passenger's seat, then started the engine.

Once out of the compound, Meg called Sharon, who picked up immediately.

"Are you home?"

"Sure am," responded Sharon.

"Great, I'm on my way over."

* * *

"I'M PRETTY sure he has a personality disorder, or is using some sort of marine style psychological warfare on Lucille. That woman has lost her marbles saying the things she said."

Sharon led Meg to the living room and gently steered her into one of the wingback chairs that faced a bay window with a view of Serenity Beach. It was the equivalent to a therapist's couch.

"I'm sure she didn't mean it. She was speaking for Allan and not herself."

Meg shook her head." But Allan isn't even in town. We

were there alone. He's got her hooked on something. I don't know what it is. Maybe she's not really my mother and the real Lucille is locked away in a bunker."

Sharon gave a polite smile. "Meg, listen to what you're saying. I think you're being a little extreme."

"I'm sure you're right, but it's irritating how she references Allan and treats him like he matters more than I do."

Sharon patted Meg's shoulder. "Well, they are married and, Meg, you may feel that way soon."

"About who? Brandon? That'll never happen."

"What do you mean?"

"We broke up. I broke up with him. It was the best thing to do and besides, I think he was seeing someone else."

"How do you know?"

Meg opened her mouth to answer when the doorbell rang. Sharon held up her finger. "Hold that thought." Sharon walked over to the door and opened it as if she were expecting someone.

"Hey, Sharon. These were my last ones, I hope you can use them," said Ciara. Meg turned toward the door and felt a small panic. Did Sharon invite her over intentionally?

Ciara stepped into the foyer. "Come into the living room. Meg's here too."

"Hey, Megs, what are you two up to?"

"Nothing much. Sharon's been listening to me rant about Lucille and Sergeant Allan."

"Oh, really? How is Lucille?"

"She's doing great; doing Allan's bidding," Megan snarked.

Sharon gestured toward the sofa. "Ciara, sit down. I baked some cookies for the guests and have some leftovers. I'll bring them in."

"Okay. I can't stay long, I have to get back to The Blue Lobster before the dinner rush is over."

Sharon left the room. Ciara sat on a sofa that faced the same direction as Meg's wing chair. Meg shifted toward her.

"So, how's the day going?"

"The usual. We've been busy and I'm actually looking forward to the end of the season. I always seem to feel this way about this far into the summer."

"How about you? Still taking the job in New Hampshire?"

Meg bit her bottom lip and was about to answer when Sharon returned with a plate of cookies. Meg looked at Sharon and said, "I'm not taking it."

"Really? You decided it was too far after all, huh? Good for you. I probably wouldn't take it either," said Ciara.

Sharon put the plate and a stack of napkins on the table between them, then sat across from the two. Ciara took one of the cookies and bit it. "These are really good, Sharon. Would you be willing to share the recipe? I could make them a special on my menu."

"Sure. I'll send it over. It's just a recipe I found online, happy to share it."

Meg took a napkin and a cookie. "Mmm, these are good. Include me in the email too."

"So, now that you're not taking the job in New Hampshire, what's your plan?"

Meg shifted in her seat, then put the cookie down on the table. Sharon caught her eye then nodded. "I... uh, had another job offer and think I'm going to take it."

"Wow! That's great. Is it nearby?"

"Yep, right here in Bluewater. In fact, further down Main Street, based at the town hall."

Ciara finished her cookie then wiped her chocolate stained fingers on a napkin. "Town hall? What are you going to be doing there?"

Sharon got up and moved closer to Meg.

"I'll be working for the mayor."

Ciara's brows furrowed. She looked down at the napkin in her hand. "What do you mean? My brother?"

Sharon straightened and moved in closer. "Ciara, Meg needed a job and for her to leave town and sell her home is more than she wanted to do and we want what's best for Meg, right?"

Ciara looked at the pair. "Sharon, you knew about this? Have you two been talking about this behind my back? I thought we were friends."

Sharon got up and sat on the sofa between Meg and Ciara. "It's not like that …"

"Oh, it is like that and of all the jobs listed in the paper you applied to the one offered by the mayor. You two know our history."

"Ciara, I needed a job, and he offered one to me. I don't see anything wrong with that."

Ciara moved away from Sharon. "And then you called me over here to break the news to me like I'm some sort of hostile. I see what's going on here. It's always been the two of you against irrational me. Well, I'm not buying it today and good luck with my rat for a brother."

Meg closed her eyes and wished she'd stayed home today. Ciara stood, then headed for the door.

"Ciara, wait, let's finish talking about this." Sharon leaped up.

"Oh, I think we're done talking. Thanks for the cookies," she said before walking through the door.

Meg looked up at Sharon and with a half-smile said, "Thanks for trying to help." Meg stood too and hugged Sharon.

"I'm sorry," Sharon said.

"Don't worry about it. I'm going to head out. We'll talk later."

The pair walked to the door, defeated.

"I'm sure once Ciara cools off she'll see things differently," Sharon said. Meg shrugged her shoulders and walked onto the porch

"It really doesn't matter at this point, but thanks again." Meg made her way down the steps. The sun warmed her face, and it was still a perfect day to stop by the beach.

She needed a quiet space to collect her thoughts and respond to Kevin's offer. Serenity Beach was a good place.

22

Meg stepped onto the beach and removed her sandals. She scrunched her toes and let them sink into the warm, grainy sand. Meg held the rolled blanket under her arm as she made her way to the shoreline.

Waves rolled in and out marking the shore with lines of foam. Meg inhaled the salty air and smiled as the almost warm water washed over her toes. She resisted the urge to wade into the bay and would dive in without question if she'd worn her bathing suit.

Meg made her way to a dry patch of sand away from shoreline and spread the blanket. She sat down, stretched her legs and leaned back on her hands. It was a light beach crowd which made it more peaceful than usual. She'd have space to think.

Meg pulled her water bottle from her bag and tipped it back for a drink. In her peripheral vision, she saw someone sitting about a hundred feet to her left. She turned, then smiled. Meg picked up her blanket and trudged over.

"Hey, Brandon, taking advantage of the weather?"

Brandon jerked his head up from his phone. His eyes widened in surprise.

"Meg, Hey what are you doing here?" Brandon's voice squeaked.

"The same as you. I wanted to get in some beach time. It's a gorgeous day."

Brandon put his phone away and peeked around Meg toward the seawall. She followed his gaze, then down beside his blanket. A set of women's sandals sat beside his flip-flops. Her chest tensed and she shifted her eyes to wipe them.

So, he's not alone. It's probably where's his attention has been lately.

Meg pushed her shoulders back. No, she wasn't going to make any assumptions. Besides, they weren't a couple anymore and he wasn't her problem.

"Are you here with someone?"

"Well, yeah, but you broke up with me, remember?" His voice was accusing.

"I was just asking. Anyone I know?"

Brandon shrugged. His shoulders hung near his ears from obvious tension.

"Relax, I'm not here to cause trouble."

His eyes darted between Meg and something behind her. She turned again to see a young woman approaching. Brandon pushed himself up and brushed the sand from his hands.

"Ashley, this is Megan. Megan, this is Ashley."

Megan's eyes grew wide. It was the purple flower sweater girl.

Ashley put out her hand and squinted at Megan. "Nice to meet you. Haven't we met before?"

Yes, they met several times. In the elevator—twice. Was she that forgetful?

"Yes, we have. In the elevator down at the district office.

You were wearing my sweater. Well, not my actual sweater, but I have one just like it."

Brandon flushed. "Oh, you two have met? What a coincidence?"

Meg glared at Brandon, who shifted his gaze toward the sand.

"That's right, we met at the district offices. Wait, Megan… Megan Hollis?"

"Yes, that's me. How do you know my name?"

"Uh, Ashley, we better get going. Our dinner reservation is coming up soon and…"

"What are you talking about, Brandon? We don't need reservations for Applebee's."

Megan covered her mouth to hide her smirk. Brandon loved a cheap date or she didn't know he was tightwad.

"Your name came up in one of our meetings as a rehire, but Brandon said he was pretty certain you had a job already and recommended we rehire the next person on the list."

Meg's jaw tensed. "Oh really?"

Brandon avoided her stare and found interest in picking up the shells near his feet.

"I'm sorry we didn't have a chance to work together. Your résumé was packed with a lot of great experience. I hope you're enjoying your current job."

"I haven't started my new job yet, but I'm sure I'll like it."

Brandon's shell collecting took him a ways down the beach.

"Well, it was nice meeting you, Ashley. Enjoy Applebee's."

Ashley smirked, then rolled her eyes. "Sure, I guess. It was nice meeting you too, Megan."

Megan wanted to yell "good bye, loser" to Brandon, but knew he'd get what was coming to him. Not only was he a cheat, but a liar that caused her job loss. She wanted to be angry, but knew it wouldn't help or change things. She needed to get back to Kevin.

The sun lowered in the horizon, and the water seemed to lap against it. She checked her watch and decided to find another spot further down Serenity Beach. Megan felt a new urgency. If Kevin gave the job to someone else, Meg would have no other choice than to leave Bluewater.

Meg pulled out her phone and dialed Kevin's number.

* * *

"Hello, you've reached the voicemail of Kevin McDougal, your friendly neighborhood mayor. Unfortunately, I'm not able to talk right now, but your call is important to me. So, leave a message and I'll get back to you."

Meg's stomach fluttered listening to Kevin's message. She felt her lips turn up into a slow smile.

"Hello, my friendly neighborhood mayor. I'm returning your call and hoping you haven't filled the position. Things have changed, and I'd be happy to work for you. So give me a call when you get a chance. By the way it's me, Meg."

Kevin gave Meg his personal number. She didn't want to assume anything, but that meant something. She wasn't sure what or how much, but she'd find out.

Meg tucked the phone into her purse, crossed her legs, then leaned back on her arms. A couple passed by holding hands and laughing while a small cocker spaniel ran ahead of them. She thought of her and Kevin.

The sun dipped a little lower as a breeze kicked up, carrying the salty scent of the Atlantic across Meg's face. This was her safe place, her home, and she'd do what was necessary to stay.

Meg breathed in the salt water breezes. She weighed her options to stay a little longer and watch the sunset or get home before dark to make a meal of noodles. It wasn't a tough choice.

She felt the vibration of her phone. Meg reached into her bag. Kevin's name flashed across the screen.

"Hi, Kevin, I just called."

"I saw that. Sorry I couldn't pick up line, but I heard your message."

Meg gripped the phone and gently bit her lip. "So, is the job still available?"

Kevin paused. "I'm sorry, Meg, I was pushed to fill it and it just happened, but I know of another position here and the person who's hiring is a friend. If you get your résumé to me today, I'll walk it over to him and put in a good word. Unfortunately, it's a part-time position, at least for now."

Meg sighed. "Thanks, I would appreciate that and I'll send my résumé over now. Please, let your friend know I'll take the job if there's an offer."

"Will do, Meg, and again, I'm sorry about the job. I'll have him get back to you as soon as possible."

"Thanks." Meg hung up the line and searched for her résumé on her phone, then emailed it to Kevin. She tucked the phone back in the bag, then pulled her legs into her chest. If she could kick herself, she would. Now she had to wait to hear back about another job. The sun was setting and cooler winds blew in from the bay. Meg pulled the blanket around her shoulders.

A part-time job was better than no job, but it also meant a cut in pay. Meg would have to figure out a way to earn more money. Half a paycheck would not pay the mortgage.

If she had only accepted the job from the start. At least she didn't have to worry about Ciara and her attitude since she'd no longer be working for Kevin.

Meg took one last look along the beach. Most of the families had packed up and left. It was the dinner hour. Her stomach grumbled, and she wondered what was on the menu at The Blue Lobster.

Meg stood and stretched her arms up, then gathered her things. "Time to get home."

She strolled to the car and climbed in. Her phone dinged an email alert. Kevin made good on his promise and his friend made her an offer with a salary attached. Meg blinked twice. It was much lower than she expected and as much as she wanted to stay in her townhome, the salary made it obvious it was no longer a possibility.

Meg started the engine and backed out of the space to drive back to the house that she'd have to leave.

23

Trixie met Meg at the door as per their usual routine. Meg scooped her into her arms, then rubbed her furry head.

"How was your day?"

Trixie purred, then licked Megs fingers.

"Hungry, girl?"

Meg released her and Trixie leaped to the floor. She followed Meg into the kitchen.

"You really liked the fancy food I bought, your bowl is clean."

Meg opened the cabinet door, got out another can and spooned it into Trixie's dish. She paced behind Meg until she finished and stepped out of the way. Trixie gobbled up her meal, not looking up till her dish was licked clean. Meg hoped her next place would have enough space for Trixie's things and for her to roam around. It would most likely be an apartment. A pang of guilt struck Meg. Her feline baby had become accustomed to the freedoms of living in a townhome. Its surrounding green space had become part of her playground. She knew Trixie would adapt, but it didn't help Meg feel better about the inevitable move.

Meg went to her desk. Piles of paper covered the entire surface. It became a catchall since she stopped working. Meg pulled out the single drawer and searched for a calculator.

"Found it."

Meg sat at the desk and pushed the paper pile aside. She plugged in different figures and thought of different scenarios that would allow them to stay in the home, but each result showed a number worse than the prior.

Her heart grew heavy. The beginnings of a headache formed, so she put the calculator back in the drawer and walked to the kitchen for a glass of water.

Meg took out a frozen meal and put it into the microwave. She rarely ate the frozen dinners since they were a reminder of her youth, which were lean times for her family. But she had to do what she had to do right now.

It seemed like she slipped back into those days, despite having done all of the right things. All the things her mother didn't do, yet she stood on the brink of homelessness. The timer sounded. Meg removed her meal, spooned it on a plate, and headed to the sanctity of her sofa. Trixie retreated to the top of her cat tree, where she watched Meg blow on her food while swaying her tail.

Meg flicked on the TV to catch up on her favorite show when her phone vibrated. She set the plate down on the sofa table and got the phone from her purse. Sharon's avatar flashed on the screen.

"Hi, Sharon." Meg put the phone on speaker.

"I'm calling to see how you're feeling. I'm really sorry about what happened here earlier today. I had no idea it would turn out that way."

"Don't worry about it, it's not your fault. Ciara and I have to resolve it.

"That's true, but I should not have pushed it."

"Really, Sharon, don't beat yourself up about it. I think we'll be fine when I tell her I won't be working for Kevin, after all."

"What happened?"

"Well, don't say anything, but he filled the position before I returned his call."

"That was crappy of him. I can't believe he'd do that after promising the job to you."

"It really wasn't his fault. I turned him down before he called again to offer it a second time. He had to fill it and I called him back too late, that's all."

"It still stinks though. So, what are you going to do? And, Meg, why don't you let me help you. It's not a problem and you can take as long as you want to pay me back."

"Thanks, Sharon. I appreciate your offer and I may need a favor."

"Anything, what do you need?"

"Well, as it turns out, Kevin forwarded my résumé to a friend who had a position open for a part-time administrator. I got the job, but the salary is half of what I made with the library. So, after crunching the numbers, I'm still going to sell the house, but will need a place to stay until I can build enough savings for a rent deposit. Can I stay at the Inn?" Meg held her breath, waiting for a response. She didn't want to assume Sharon's answer.

"Of course you can stay."

Meg exhaled. "Thank you, Sharon. I really do appreciate your help."

"Not that it matters, but after selling the house, won't you have a lump sum of money to use toward your new place?"

Meg shrugged her shoulders. "Actually, I won't. There's no equity in the house."

"Oh, I see. Well, like I said, you're welcome to stay and for as long as you need."

"Great! I promise that Trixie will not be a problem either."

Sharon paused then said, "Meg, I'm sorry, but did you forget? I'm allergic to cats."

Trixie jumped down from the top of her cat tree and leaped onto the sofa next to Meg. She rubbed her furry head.

Tears rimmed Meg's eyes "Oh, I forgot about that. Sure, it's not a problem. I'll just have to find a place for her to go in the meantime."

Trixie pushed her head in to Meg's hand for a deeper rub. She cuddled the calico on her lap.

"I'm sorry, Meg. You know I'd let her come if it weren't for my allergies."

"Of course, I know that. I'll find a nice place for her to go. Well, I better get off the phone, my dinner is getting cold."

"Okay, we'll talk more later. Bye Meg."

"Thanks Sharon, bye now."

Meg placed the phone face down on the coffee table. Her chest heaved and a cascade of tears flowed. She held Trixie close to her chest like an infant.

"Trixie girl, I'm going to find you the best place." She said, her voice cracking. Somewhere you can roam freely, play and be loved."

Trixie meowed and pushed away from Meg. She dashed to the bedroom.

"Trixie! I'm sorry."

Meg stood and carried her cold plate of food to the trash can and dumped it inside. She needed to find a family to adopt Trixie. She wished Lucille could keep her, but there was no way Allan would allow a non-compliant animal in his house. She'd start her search online. Meg put on a sweater to get her laptop from the car.

She jogged to the car, opened the trunk, and took out her

computer bag. Meg slammed the trunk shut. A chilling howl came from the woods behind her townhouse. The coyotes were out. She trotted back to the door which she left slightly ajar and walked back in the house.

Meg took out the laptop, and placed it on the desk. She typed in "cat adoptions". Over half a million hits came up. Meg closed the computer.

"Not tonight." She said, then stuffed the laptop back in the bag.

Meg walked up to the bedrooms and called, "Trixie! Trixie! Where are you, girl? I've got a treat for you."

She came back down to the kitchen and pulled out a bag of her favorite chewy treats. The sound of the wrapper always sent Trixie tearing around the corner into the kitchen. Meg crinkled the bag a second time, but no Trixie. She put the bag on the counter and checked Trixie's hiding places. She wasn't there. Was she that upset and really avoiding Meg?

"Trixie!" Meg called out again, then stopped at the front door. Her mind flashed to the open door while she went to the car for her laptop. Did Trixie slip out?

Meg rushed around the house looking in every closet, nook and crevice. It was as if she disappeared. She stood in the middle of her bedroom floor and realized Trixie was no longer in the house. Howls rose from the rear of the property. Megan cried out, "Trixie, the coyotes!"

24

Meg ran to the front door and flung it open. She tromped to the rear of the townhomes, barely able to make out the shadows in the darkness. Clouds blanketed the evening sky, making it harder than usual to see.

Just beyond the brush leading into the line of trees, sets of glowing eyes crouched low and watched Meg intently. She quivered as if of icicles trickled down her spine. Low growls hung in the tall grass.

She'd never been face-to-face with a pack of coyotes. Meg froze. She wanted to run, but her feet wouldn't move. "Don't show fear, don't show fear," she whispered to herself. "Back away, back away." Her feet obeyed.

One of the coyotes broke from the pack and approached her. Meg continued to back up while keeping her eyes on the crouching animal. Her heart pounded as her breath quickened.

"Go away doggie, I'm the boss," she shouted. Meg took two steps backward. Her foot landed on a rock and she lost her balance. She fell to the ground and saw the coyote trot in her direction.

Meg jumped up, grabbed the rock, and hurled it at the fearless animal. A loud yelp confirmed she'd hit her target. Meg scanned the shadowy tree line and saw the tail of a single coyote retreat into the woods.

She shuddered at how close she'd been to an attack. While she knew coyotes normally preyed on other animals, attacks on humans wasn't an unheard of event. Meg peered farther into the woods, but still no sign of Trixie. Her fear returned as quickly as it left.

Meg tracked back to the house for a flashlight and on her way tumbled down a small hill. Her scraped knee trickled blood. She sat in a heap, feeling sorry for herself, and held it.

Meg held it as long as she could until the tears streamed down her face; her chest heaved. She curled into a quivering ball then gave way to a sob that released the whole of her emotions.

She sobbed for getting furloughed; she cried for losing her job and wept about how she'd been a fool about Brandon. Meg bawled that she was losing her home and one of her best friends. And now, worst of all, Trixie had run away into the night, unprotected from the danger of coyotes.

Her head pounded, and her heart hurt with the stress of multiple losses. Meg wrapped her arms tighter around herself and rocked to push away the pain.

Meg sat in a heap until her cries turned to a whimper and she knew that self-pity would not get Trixie back to safety.

Meg unfurled her body and pushed herself to standing then dragged herself inside. She needed help and called the one person she had always relied on.

* * *

LENA PEARSON

The phone rang several times.

"Hello, Meg?"

"Mom, Mom, I need your help."

"What's wrong, honey?"

"Trixie ran away. She's outside somewhere and the coyotes are out. What if they catch her?" Meg's throat tightened.

"I'm on my way."

Meg put the phone down and searched for another flashlight, then stuffed her pocket full of chewy cat treats. She paced the room, thinking of other things she could do to help locate Trixie.

"Maybe if she heard the bell from that annoying cat ball," Meg said, then stooped to search under the couch. She tossed it in the bag with the flashlights, then emptied the treats from her pockets and put them into the bag too.

Meg walked to the front door and peeked out the window. "What's taking Lucille so long? What was I thinking to call her? It'll be just the two of us, and her eyesight is just as bad as mine." Meg crossed her arms. "We're going to need more help," she said and reached for her phone when the doorbell rang, followed by a series of knocks. Meg swung the door open.

"Mom, what—"

"Hey, Meg, we heard you needed some help looking for Trixie," Ciara said. Sharon stepped from behind and shook a bottle of Zyrtec allergy medicine. "I'm ready for the search," Sharon added with a smile.

"What are you two doing here?" Meg said and pulled them in for a hug.

"It's not just us. We brought a whole search team," Ciara said and pointed behind her to several cars in the parking lot that flicked their headlights.

Meg covered her mouth, then shook her head in disbelief. "How did you know... who told you?"

Ciara pointed to Sharon who said, "Well, your mother called and told me about Trixie and the panic in your voice. She asked if I could help. So, I called Ciara because I knew she'd want to be here too."

Ciara turned to Meg. "And she's right. Through hell and..." she paused, and they each chimed in, "Bluewater!"

A series of barks and howls sobered the moment. Meg grabbed her bag and stepped outside. She closed the door behind her, then led Ciara and Sharon to the parking lot.

The doors to the waiting cars opened and let out a group of familiar faces. They walked up to the trio. Meg recognized a few from Ciara's staff, a couple of the restaurant regulars, and two of Sharon's staff from the Inn. Meg's heart was full. Kevin stepped out of the last car and walked up to the crowd.

"Is there space for one more?"

Meg turned to Ciara. "He was at our mother's house when the call came in, and he overheard. Trust me, I didn't invite him."

"She's right. I hope it's okay." His bright eyes met Meg's. Her stomach fluttered, and she turned away.

She loved her friends and didn't expect this response.

"We better get started," Ciara said

"Where was the last place you saw him?" one of the searchers asked.

"What does he look like?" said another.

"She's a calico with orange and black spots. Her name is Trixie. The last place I saw her was in the house, but she's not there. I'm certain she ran out when I went to my car."

"Do you have any idea where she might have gone?" asked Kevin.

Meg pointed to the left of her townhouse toward the dark woods. "I have a couple of flashlights." Meg gave one to

Sharon and the other to Kevin, whose fingers grazed hers. A trickle of electricity tingled her tips and traveled the length of her arm. She pulled her hand back as if she'd actually gotten an electric shock. Had he felt it too?

"We're going to need more than that," said Ciara

Meg glanced around. "More of what?" she asked.

Ciara pointed to the flashlight she had in her hand. "I hope you don't think we're going to see through that dark brush with those."

As if on cue, a large dark tank like vehicle rolled into the parking lot. Meg couldn't believe it. The enormous thing parked beside Meg's car; the door opened and Lucille popped out. "Hey, honey!"

"Mom? Why are you driving Allan's tank?"

"You'd be amazed at what this thing can do?"

"Oh, really? Does it come with flashlights?"

"I've got something better." Lucille ducked back into the truck and seconds later large search lights flooded the back woods like it was daytime. The search crew cheered.

"Now let's go and find our Trixie," Sharon said.

Lucille jumped down from the truck with a spryness that surprised Meg.

"Wow, Mom, that's impressive and thanks for coming out."

"You're welcome, dear."

"Also, thank you for calling my friends over."

"No thanks necessary. I knew we couldn't get this done on our own, so let's get started."

Lucille looked down to Meg's bloody knee.

"What happened there?"

"Let's just say I had a moment, but I'm over it now. Maybe I'll tell you later."

Meg and Lucille trudged up the hill toward the woods, guided by the wide spread of light from the tank. A flash of movement sent the searchers over to an area near the edge of the woods.

"False alarm!" one of them called out

"Let's spread out and form a single line while approaching the tree line and into the woods," Kevin directed.

The group followed his lead and formed a line that spanned half the length of the shadowy cluster of trees. They all walked in unison, scanning the grounds and any suspicious movements. Meg's heart pounded wildly in her chest. So much time had passed and still no sign of Trixie. She pushed the worst of her thoughts to the back of her mind and forged ahead.

"Trixie girl, where are you?" she mumbled to herself, then took out her favorite bell ball and shook it. A hollow jingle came from the ball. Meg wiped a tear from her cheek.

25

Step by step, the searchers entered the dark brush. The lights from the tank began to fade the deeper they traveled. Soon the line broke down into clusters being led by folks with flashlights.

Low branches smacked Meg and blocked her path. Pine sap glued needles to the soles of her shoes and filled her nostrils with the astringent smell.

"Meg, how are you holding up?" Sharon whispered from her left.

"As best I can. I hope we can find her tonight. It's so dark out here. Without the flashlight, it's hard to see anything beyond my hand."

Sharon patted Meg on the shoulder. "You're right, it's very dark."

A group of searchers to the far right stopped and gathered around a spot. There was a low whistle followed by an, "Oh man." Meg rushed to where they stood and pointed her flashlight on the ground.

She shook her head over and over, muttering, "No, no, no." Meg collapsed to the ground and dropped her flashlight next to a pile of mangled fur and blood.

Her tears turned to heavy sobs. Sharon knelt down and embraced her. "I'm so sorry, Meg. So, so, sorry."

"Let's get her to the house," said Lucille

"No, we can't leave her here alone. I have to take her," Meg insisted.

"Sure, we'll get someone else to do it. You're in no shape right now to do that," Lucille said and helped Meg to her feet.

Sharon told the rest that the search was over. The groups disbanded and walked out of the woods toward the search lights.

Sharon caught up with Lucille and Meg. She walked on the other side while patting Meg's back. Lucille called Kevin over and whispered in his ear. He went to the tank and walked back to the brush with a box and a flashlight.

"I'll go and help him find her," Sharon said to Lucille, then trotted behind him.

One by one, each of the searchers offered Meg their condolences and words of sympathy. Several minutes later they got into their cars and drove away.

She would not have guessed the night would end this way. Her chest ached. Meg stepped on the front step leading to the door when Trixie's hollow ball bell rang in her pocket. Meg crumpled to the ground and cried. Lucille wrapped her arms around Meg and rocked with her.

"What's going on?" Ciara said, stepping from inside the townhouse. At the same time Sharon and Kevin came around the corner with wide grins holding the box. They stopped at the sight of Ciara.

"Look who I found," Ciara said. A low purr caused Meg and Lucille to turn around. Ciara held Trixie in her arms and rubbed her head, making her purr louder.

"I came in to use the john and she ran into the house after

me. And so I scooped her up and told her she'd been a bad kitty."

Meg jumped up and took Trixie from Ciara.

"No, not a bad kitty, just sad. She knew I had plans to give her away, and that's probably why she left. I'm sorry, Trixie."

"Well, now that she is safe and sound, I guess we can bring these remains to animal control," Sharon said, and they all looked at her.

"That was going to be our good news." Kevin looked down at the box. "Well, kinda. These are raccoon remains. It looks like the coyotes got into a fight with it and unfortunately the raccoon lost."

Trixie squirmed under Meg's hug.

"I'm happy Trixie is back," said Sharon, who gave her a light pat on the head before sneezing.

"I better turn off those lights and get home. Allan's coming back tomorrow and I'm picking him up from Logan airport in the morning," said Lucille.

Meg reached for her mother's hand. "Thanks, Mom, I'll call you tomorrow afternoon."

"You're welcome, dear." Lucille leaned over and gave Meg a peck on the cheek. She stood and dusted off her jeans, then walked over to the big tank. Lucille climbed into the oversized vehicle and soon rode off.

"Well, I better get going too. It's been a long day and I've got an early day at The Blue Lobster tomorrow," said Ciara.

"I have to leave too. Ciara's my ride. We'll talk tomorrow, okay. Meg?"

"Sure, Sharon, and thanks Ciara. You two are the best."

"Well, we can't argue with that, right, Sharon?" They all laughed, then hugged. Meg pulled away from the group and looked at Ciara. "So we're good now?"

"Yep, all good." They hugged once more.

"We better get going," said Sharon

Ciara pointed to Kevin then whispered to Meg, "Make sure you-know-who doesn't stay too long."

"I heard you, Ciara," Kevin said

"That was the point," said Ciara.

Kevin ran one hand through his thick curls, then put the box down to avoid eye contact with his sister. Ciara smirked.

"Thanks, Ciara. I'll be fine. You and Sharon better go, it's late."

"Okay, Megs. We'll talk later." Ciara gave Kevin one last sneer before walking to the car where Sharon was waiting. They got in, pulled out of the parking spot, and headed down the road.

Kevin gestured toward the empty parking space. "Sorry about that."

"No, don't apologize. I know you and Ciara have your issues, but she's still my friend."

"Right." Kevin nodded his head.

"It's a little chilly out here. Do you want to come inside?"

"No, but thank you. I just wanted to be sure you were okay. It was a pretty scary night. I didn't know the coyotes were that serious."

Meg shivered and walked to the door. She opened it and put Trixie inside, careful to close it firmly, then turned back to Kevin.

"They are. Every night I hear them out here in packs, howling and running around. It's more than disturbing."

Meg wrapped her arms around herself. Kevin took off his jacket. "Here, take this," he said and drape it over Meg. It smelled like a spicy aftershave.

"Thank you."

They sat down in front of Meg's door inches apart from each other.

"I think I'm going to include the coyote problem in my platform… you know, for the next election."

"Oh, really? Another promise?"

"I guess, but this time it's personal," said Kevin.

"I'm sure. There's nothing like seeing what they can do to an innocent creature up close." Meg gestured to the box a few feet away.

"Right and for the safety of the citizens."

"That's a good promise—to keep people safe." Meg smiled and glanced at him. He caught her eye. Her face warmed under his gaze.

"Yes, to keep you safe," he whispered.

The hairs on her arms prickled. She could feel his leg on hers.

"Meg?"

She turned and answered with a hushed, "Yes." And he was there. His warm breath on her face. She leaned in and pushed her lips into his. He parted his lips and pulled her into his arms, returning the kiss. Meg's heart raced.

Kevin took her hand and pulled her up. They stood facing each other. He leaned in and kissed her again, holding her close. Meg's head swirled. She felt special, safe, and wanted.

He pulled back. His fingers trailed down her cheeks to her lips, outlining the shape of her mouth. A shiver ran through her whole body, making her tremble. Kevin brushed his mouth over hers. She ached for more, but knew it had already gone too far.

"Kevin, we can't do this," she whispered.

He stepped back and shook his head. "I know, you're right. I should go."

"It's probably best." Meg slipped off his jacket and handed it to him.

Kevin took it and backed down the steps nearly falling. Meg covered her mouth to hide a giggle.

"Thanks, Meg. I'll be around. Call me if you need anything."

Meg pointed to the box.

"Oh right." Kevin jogged back up the steps and grabbed the box of mangled raccoon. He grimaced when he held it, as it started to smell bad.

"Thanks, Kevin."

"No problem."

Meg watched him open the trunk and place the box in there. She waved, then went into the house. Trixie sat on the couch waving her tail in the air as if she had a story to tell.

26

The boxes were stacked alongside the wall in the kitchen. Meg had more stuff stored away in cabinets and closets than she realized. Packing boxes took up most of her morning. She planned to pack a few more boxes before moving them to the guest bedroom, then taking a lunch break.

Meg spent the earlier part of the day talking to a realtor that Lucille recommended. She felt confident that she could get a fair price for the townhouse. Enough to pay the mortgage and fees associated with the house sale.

She worked so hard to have a place of her own, only to be selling it and starting over again. It surprised her how she made a plan for what needed to be done and actually did it. How did she ever think she could rely on Brandon for her job or expect a handout from her mom without questions?

Meg knew the answers and promised to trust her abilities when life got hard. It felt good to depend on herself, despite having no idea about her tomorrows. The difference this time was Meg trusted she would get through it.

One thing she wasn't so certain about getting through

was finding a home for Trixie. She spent most of the day hiding from Meg, and Meg couldn't blame her. She was sure Trixie knew her fate, and if that door opened again, she would take another shot at leaving.

Meg held off on making the phone call while in the house. Maybe she'd call some of the classifieds at Lucille's—away from Trixie. Meg packed one more box, then topped off her bowl with her favorite treat in an effort to lure her from hiding. She shook her favorite toy, which at least caused her to poke her head from beneath the couch.

"Come on, Trixie girl. Are you going to hide from me all day?"

Trixie retreated back under the sofa.

"Ugh!" Meg rolled the ball under the couch. The bell in the ball rang as she assumed Trixie swiped it with her paws out of Meg's sight.

"That's fine. I have other things I can do besides wait for you to come from out of there."

She picked up a box and carried it to the bedroom and came back for another. As she leaned over, the doorbell rang, followed by a few knocks. Meg stood and walked to the door.

"Hey, Ciara," she said before the door was fully open.

Ciara's hand hung in the air, poised for another knock. Her eyes squinted. "How'd you know it was me?"

Meg opened the door wider and stepped to the side to allow Ciara in.

"You have a unique knock. If you didn't own the restaurant, I'd recommend the police force to you." They both laughed.

"I've heard my hands are a little heavy."

She closed the door behind her and walked back to the kitchen. Ciara followed.

"What's with all the boxes?"

"I'm moving. I told you already. Did you forget?"

Ciara stuck her hands in her pockets. "Well, no. I guess I didn't believe you. So you're really selling the place?"

"Yup, I have no choice. My new job at the town hall doesn't pay as much as my old job and so I'm putting the house on the market. I'll be moving into one of the rooms at Sharon's Inn."

"Really? I didn't know all of that?"

"Well, you were too upset for us to tell you. So now you know." Meg picked up a box and handed it to Ciara, then took a second one and headed down the hall to the second bedroom. Ciara did the same.

"I wish you'd told me then maybe we could have figured something out. I should have known that my cheapskate brother couldn't pay you well, it's just like him."

Meg put the box on the floor, then took the second one from Ciara and stacked it on top of the first. She turned to Ciara and put her hands on her hips. "Well, Ciara, your brother's job actually paid better than my last job, but I waited too long and he had to fill it. And because of him, I'm employed, but just not working for him. That should make you feel better."

Ciara stared down at her hands, non-responsive. Meg walked past her out of the room.

"Look, I know my brother did you a favor, but we're still friends and I'd like to help too."

Meg shrugged her shoulder. "Well, I could use another part-time job. Do you have any wait positions at The Blue Lobster Grill?"

Ciara took a couple of steps back and pressed her lips together.

"It's okay. You don't have to hire me. I can find something else in town."

Ciara lifted her palms and waved them. "No, it's not that

at all. I have another idea, but you'll need to come to the restaurant this evening. In fact, both you and Sharon need to be there."

"Sure. what's it all about?"

"I can't tell you now. You just need to be there."

"Sure, I'll be there. What time?"

"Nine o'clock is good, both you and Sharon. Will you call her for me?"

Meg nodded her head. She planned to use the time to do more packing, but it sounded important to Ciara.

"Great! Well, I better get back to the restaurant. And I'll see you there later?"

Meg nodded and watched Ciara look around the living room.

"Where's Trixie?"

"Oh, she's hiding from me under the couch."

"Really? She seems like a lot of work."

"No, it's not that. She's been upset since yesterday and that's probably why she ran out the house."

Ciara furrowed her brows. Meg leaned in and whispered, "I think she knows we're leaving and I can't take her with me to Sharon's because of her allergies. So, I have to find a home for her."

"Oh, wow. I get it now." Ciara blew out a slow breath, then turned to let herself out.

"I'll see you this evening," said Meg.

"Yup, see you then."

Meg made sure the door was securely closed, then peeked under the sofa. Glowing green eyes peered back at her, then looked away.

"Trixie, how long are you going to hold this grudge? It's getting old."

Meg's phone vibrated. She stood up and scooped it from the sofa table.

"Hello?"

A warm baritone answered back and her stomach fluttered. "Hey, Meg, it's me, Kevin. Are you busy?"

She put the phone on speaker, then held the phone close. "No, not really. I was trying to coax Trixie from her hiding place, but no luck. So, how are you?" Images of last night's kiss came to her mind along with the memories of his spicy scent.

"I, uh, was thinking about us... I mean, you and the job. I hope you're not offended, but I asked my friend about his offer and he told me what you accepted. Please don't take this the wrong way, but it was an incredibly low salary."

"No, I'm not offended. It is low, but it's a job and keeps me in the area."

"Well, I feel partly responsible for you having to take it and started thinking about all the help I'll need for my upcoming campaign. Would you be interested in working for me in a paid position doing research? There's no competition and the hours are flexible."

"Sure, I'll definitely consider it. What kind of research?"

"Oh, Meg, can I get back to you. My colleague walked in for a meeting, but take your time. Like I said, there's no competition. I just texted you the salary. Sound good?"

Meg could hear the rush in his voice and she was curious about the amount he texted.

"Yes, thanks, Kevin. I'll talk to you later."

"Okay, bye now," Kevin said and got off the line.

Meg navigated to her texts and tapped on Kevin's name. She gasped and stiffened at the figure. Meg didn't have to do the math. If she took the job, Meg and Trixie didn't have to move. She wanted to call him right away and scream, "Yes! I'll take it!" but he was in a meeting and she needed to show some restraint. So she texted back in all caps, "I'll take it!"

He responded with a thumbs-up and a happy emoji face.

Trixie must have sensed her excitement, or maybe it was Megs bouncing on the sofa that constricted her hiding space. Whatever it was, she came out and made a beeline to her bowl in the kitchen.

Meg called out, "Trixie! I have a job!"

She ran into the kitchen and scooped her up furry baby, "And we are staying in our home."

Meg checked the wall clock. She promised Ciara she'd meet her and Sharon at the Blue Lobster. She nuzzled Trixie and put her on the floor then shook a finger at her, "I'll be gone for a couple of hours. Don't get yourself into trouble."

Meg was buoyant and couldn't wait to share the exciting news with her best friends. She grabbed her purse and keys and cast one last look at Trixie to make sure she was still there.

Her phone buzzed with a message from Sharon. "On your way?!!"

Meg responded with a thumbs up emoji. Why the urgency? And what was this idea Ciara wanted to share with the two of them? Her stomach fluttered as she headed out the door.

EPILOGUE

CIARA

The place was filled to capacity. Ciara stood at the front of the room and noticed when Meg walked in.

"Glad you could make it, Megs." She shouted playfully, causing the rows of people to look her way as she scooted to the front and found a seat next to Sharon. Simon sat on the other side. He gave her a quick wave.

Ciara smiled as she looked around the restaurant. There was an electricity permeating the air of the room. People filled all the seats of the large dining space. They chatted, laughed, and were in high spirits. Simon pushed his glasses up and stood to get the room's attention.

"Hello, friends, thank you all for coming out tonight and for being part of the task force. We have some big news to share with you. I'll let Ciara speak now."

Simon sat down and looked over to Sharon and Meg with a huge grin on his face, like he had a secret to tell, but couldn't. Ciara moved to the center of the room, then squinted. She fiddled with her hands and cleared her throat several times. Meg sat upright.

"Like Simon said, thank you for being here. I'll try to keep this short to give everyone a chance to eat and chat." Ciara glanced at the trio in the front row, then looked over the group.

Meg turned to Sharon. "What's this all about?" she asked.

"You're about to find out?" Sharon whispered back then turned her attention back to Ciara who began talking.

"During our last meeting, an agenda was presented. It outlined some of the actions we wanted to see done or addressed as it related to the coming development of our town. Some of you wanted to have political authority involved and mentioned the mayor."

Ciara paused and her jaw tensed. She was nervous about her announcement, but was excited about the chance to prove herself. She took a breath, then continued. "I actually thought it was a good idea to have political authority involved in the quest to preserve what's important to us and, I'm excited to announce my candidacy to run for mayor of Bluewater."

The room erupted with cheers, claps, and hoots. It emboldened her. She observed everyone's excitement, but saw Meg clapped with less enthusiasm. She knew that would change once Meg knew about the surprise she had for her.

"Isn't this exciting!" Sharon shouted over to Meg.

Meg nodded, clapped and offered a feeble grin. Her shoulders were hunched as if burdened. Ciara knew that Meg had other things on her mind and was anxious to show her everything was going to work out.

Ciara lifted and lowered her arms several times. "Everyone quiet down." The room eventually settled back into its pre-announcement mood.

Her heart pounded at the response from the crowd and it fueled her excitement to be running. Imagine being Mayor of

Bluewater. Ciara took a deep breath and turned her attention back to the room.

"Thank you so much for that amazing approval and acceptance of my candidacy. There are still several steps required to make me your official candidate and it starts there."

Ciara pointed to a table set up in the far corner of the room. Nancy stood there holding up a piece of paper.

"If you would like to see me run for mayor, please sign the document in the back. I need each of your signatures to help complete the paperwork necessary for me to officially run."

Another round of claps came from the crowd, followed by shouts.

"You've got my vote!"

"Mine too, Ciara."

"Yes! Ciara for mayor."

"Thank you all. Now let's sign and eat." Ciara turned around, and with the help of Sharon began removing dish covers of lobster rolls, kettle fried chips, wingettes, cobs of corn, and other Blue Lobster Grill specialties. Meg walked up to her friends.

"That was an amazing response. I had no idea this was your plan," said Meg.

"I've been mulling over it for a few weeks, but for obvious reasons didn't think it was a smart idea, until the last task force meeting." Ciara pointed to Meg. "You were there, right?"

"No, I left early, remember?"

"Well, that was the one."

Sharon wiped her hands on a napkin and pulled them into a hug. "Isn't this great? We get to work on the campaign with Ciara and save our town."

"Yeah, it's gonna be great…" Meg's voice trailed off.

Ciara turned to Meg. "In fact, I have something I wanted

to talk to you about." Ciara had it all figured out and couldn't wait to share her plan with Meg. She'd tell Sharon the details later. There was no one else she trusted more than Sharon and Meg to help her run for Mayor of Bluewater Bay.

"You two go ahead and chat. I'll work the room. Do we have a slogan?" asked Sharon.

"We do, and I'll fill you all in at our first team campaign meeting."

Sharon's eyes sparkled above her wide grin. "Okay. I'll make one up for now... Bluewater Dreaming... Vote for Hope, uh, never mind." Sharon waved her hand dismissively and danced away."

"I'd say she's excited," said Ciara.

"She should be, this was a wonderful surprise. I'm happy for you," said Meg, patting Ciara on the arm.

"Speaking about surprises, I want to ask you something. Do you have a few minutes?"

"Oh, sure."

"Come into the office. It's probably better if I show you."

* * *

CIARA OPENED HER OFFICE DOOR. She kept it neat to combat the chaos of running a restaurant. Color coordinated files stored in clear bins lined the far shelves. Each bin had a typewritten label. Ciara's desk held a laptop, family photo, small cacti, and a navy blotter in the center. She liked simplicity too.

A long dark wooden bookshelf ran the length of a window. It offered an unexpected view of a grassy patch in the rear of the restaurant. The padded office chair, upholstered in sea foam blue, added a splash of color to the cozy Zen like space.

Ciara sat down at the desk and opened up her laptop. In a

few taps she brought up what looked like a spreadsheet with lots of numbers. She waved Meg over.

"Come here, I want you to see what I did." She smiled and hoped it would be enough to keep her in town. .

Meg crouched down to get a look at the screen. "That's cool, a budget for your campaign. That's a lot of money. Have you started fundraising yet?"

"No, not yet. I had to move some things around and borrow a line from the restaurant's budget to make it work, but what I want you to see is this line here." She said and scrolled the screen up then ran her finger across one of the lines. "Read what it says."

"Paid Positions-Campaign Manager Megan Hollis."

Megan's mouth fell open. Ciara grinned with satisfaction. She succeeded in surprising her friend. "Wow, I-I don't know what to say."

"Say you'll take the position. I know it's not much, but after visiting with you today, I ran back to the office and put this line into the budget. The thought of you losing your home and Trixie was painful. Like I said, it's not a lot, but maybe you could pick up hours at the restaurant if needed."

Meg stood up and turned her back to Ciara.

"What's wrong?"

She groaned then turned back around. "Kevin offered me a position on his campaign team right before I came here. And I accepted."

Ciara's face reddened and her mind blanked before a rush of words spilled from her lips. "What? You're going to work against me with my brother?!"

Meg shook her head. "Wait, Ciara, I had no idea you were planning to run for mayor until a few minutes ago."

Ciara stood up and plunked her hands on ample hips. She huffed and pointed a finger at Meg who stepped back.

"Megs, don't you see what's going on? You can't trust him and he'll use you against me." Ciara crossed her arms over her chest. "Well, you're going to have to make a choice. Is it me or my brother?

* * *

READ THE NEXT BOOK IN THE SERIES !

Made in the USA
Monee, IL
17 April 2022